7 BILLION LIVES ARE IN DANGER.
13 STRANGERS WITH TERRIFYING NIGHTMARES.
1 ENEMY WILL STOP AT NOTHING TO DESTROY US ALL.

MY NAME IS SAM.
I AM ONE OF THE LAST THIRTEEN.
OUR BATTLE CONTINUES . . .

This one's for Benji and Cole—JP.

First American Edition 2014
Kane Miller, A Division of EDC Publishing

Text copyright © James Phelan, 2014
Cover design copyright © Scholastic Australia, 2014
Illustrations by Chad Mitchell. Design by Nicole Stofberg

First published by Scholastic Australia Pty Limited in 2014
This edition published under license from Scholastic Australia Pty Limited.

Cover photography: Blueprint © istockphoto.com/Adam Korzekwa; Parkour Tic-Tac © istockphoto.com/Willie B. Thomas; Climbing wall © istockphoto.com/microgen; Leonardo da Vinci (Sepia) © istockphoto.com/pictore; Gears © istockphoto.com/-Oxford-; Mechanical blueprint © istockphoto.com/teekid; Circuit board © istockphoto.com/Bjorn Meyer; Map © istockphoto.com/alengo; Grunge drawing © istockphoto.com/aleksandar velasevic; World map © istockphoto.com/Maksim Pasko; Internet © istockphoto.com/Andrey Prokhorov; Inside clock © istockphoto.com/LdF; Space galaxy © istockphoto.com/Sergii Tsololo; Sunset © istockphoto.com/Joakim Leroy; Blue flare © istockphoto.com/YouraPechkin; Global communication © istockphoto.com/chadive samanthakamani; Earth satellites © istockphoto.com/Alexey Popov; Girl portrait © istockphoto.com/peter zelei; Student & board © istockphoto.com/zhang bo; Young man serious © istockphoto.com/Jacob Wackerhausen; Portrait man © istockphoto.com/Alina Solovyova-Vincent; Sad expression © istockphoto.com/Shelly Perry; Content man © istockphoto.com/drbimages; Pensive man © istockphoto.com/Chuck Schmidt; Black and pink © istockphoto.com/blackwaterimages; Punk Girl © istockphoto.com/Kuzma; Woman escaping © Jose antonio Sanchez reyes/Photos.com; Young running man © Tatiana Belova/Photos.com; Gears clock © Jupiterimages/Photos.com; Young woman © Anomen/Photos.com; Explosions © Leigh Prather | Dreamstime.com; Landscape blueprints © Firebrandphotography | Dreamstime.com; Jump over wall © Ammentorp | Dreamstime.com; Mountains, CAN © Akadiusz Iwanicki | Dreamstime.com; Sphinx Bucegi © Adrian Nicolae | Dreamstime.com; Big mountains © Hoptrop | Dreamstime.com; Sunset mountains © Pklimenko | Dreamstime.com; Mountains lake © Janmika | Dreamstime.com; Blue night sky © Mack2happy | Dreamstime.com; Old writing © Empire331 | Dreamstime.com; Young man © Shuen Ho Wang | Dreamstime.com; Abstract cells © Sur | Dreamstime.com; Helicopter © Evren Kalinbacak | Dreamstime.com; Aeroplane © Rgbe | Dreamstime.com; Phrenology illustration © Mcarrel | Dreamstime.com; Abstract interior © Sur | Dreamstime.com; Papyrus © Cebreros | Dreamstime.com; Blue shades © Mohamed Osama | Dreamstime.com; Blue background © Matusciac | Dreamstime.com; Sphinx and Pyramid © Dan Breckwoldt | Dreamstime.com; Blue background2 © Cammeraydave | Dreamstime.com; Abstract shapes © Lisa Mckown | Dreamstime.com; Yellow Field © Simon Greig | Dreamstime.com; Blue background3 © Sergey Skrebnev | Dreamstime.com; Blue eye © Richard Thomas | Dreamstime.com; Abstract landscape © Crazy80frog | Dreamstime.com; Rameses II © Jose I. Soto | Dreamstime.com; Helicopter © Sculpies | Dreamstime.com; Vitruvian man © Cornelius20 | Dreamstime.com; Scarab beetle © Charon | Dreamstime.com; Eye of Horus © Charon | Dreamstime.com; Handsome male portrait © DigitalHand Studio/Shutterstock.com; Teen girl © CREATISTA/Shutterstock.com; Long Bay and Belmont Point in Tortola, British Virgin Islands © cdwheatley; Havana, Cuba © Tzooka | Dreamstime.com; Havana, Cuba © Dan Talson | Dreamstime.com; Cuba map © Marcio Silva | Dreamstime.com; Vehicles running in city © Xiye | Dreamstime.com; Canada Place, Vancouver, BC Canada © Edwin Verin | Dreamstime.com; Old elevator shaft © trekandshoot | Dreamstime.com; Security electronic door lock © Lcro77 | Dreamstime.com; Underwater cave © Belikova | Dreamstime.com; Scuba diver above underwater cave © Scuba13 | Dreamstime.com; Shipwreck Bay © Mskorpion | Dreamstime.com; Shipwreck and diver © Olga Khoroshunova | Dreamstime.com; Shipwreck beach © Happidog | Dreamstime.com; Wooden shipwreck © Andrew Jalbert | Dreamstime.com; Shipwreck © Olga Khoroshunova | Dreamstime.com; Footprints in the sand © Amy Walters | Dreamstime.com; Old iron cannon © Antonio De Azevedo Negrão | Dreamstime.com; Island of Tortola in Caribbean © Tom Dowd | Dreamstime.com; Driving at dusk © Jose Antonio Sánchez Reyes | Dreamstime.com; Mexico City © D-flo | Dreamstime.com; Cuba © istockphoto.com/rachidheffels; Looking in a gun barrel © istockphoto.com/ajansen; Athlete training © istockphoto.com/epicurean; Lava Canyon © istockphoto.com/Tammy616; Scuba diver in the Red Sea © istockphoto.com/mcrisari. Internal photography: p34, Cool blue world map © quisp65; p117, Security electronic door lock © xyno; p137, Crushed textured paper © tein79; p150, Tree trunk detail © yusufgonden.

For information contact:
Kane Miller, A Division of EDC Publishing
PO Box 470663
Tulsa, OK 74147-0663
www.kanemiller.com
www.edcpub.com
www.usbornebooksandmore.com

Library of Congress Control Number: 2013945817

Printed and bound in the United States of America
1 2 3 4 5 6 7 8 9 10
ISBN: 978-1-61067-271-9

THE LAST THIRTEEN

BOOK SIX

JAMES PHELAN

Kane Miller
A DIVISION OF EDC PUBLISHING

PREVIOUSLY

Sam and Zara are kidnapped by Hans and his henchmen and driven to an unknown location. Sam manages to untie himself and creeps along window ledges high above the street below to free Zara. Together they flee into the dawn, realizing they are now in Monaco.

Mourning the death of Pi, Eva tends to survivors at the Academy's devastated Swiss campus with Tobias. The next day, they are taken to London to recover and regroup.

In London, the Professor is targeted by a bomb, emphasizing the constant danger they are all now in. Sam heads to Brazil where he meets up with Pablo, a Councillor, who aids them in their search.

On a ferry on the Amazon River, Sam is attacked by Stella's men and in the ensuing battle is saved by Rapha, the next of the last 13. They fly an ultralight over the rain forest to a waterfall which hides an ancient city.

At the new Enterprise HQ in Amsterdam, Alex and Shiva wage war in a virtual battle which will affect the Dreamscape. Working together, they manage to push back their enemies and overcome a heavily armored Matrix.

Dodging booby traps, Sam and Rapha discover the mythical city in the clouds and Rapha finds his Gear. Before they can leave, Hans' men surround them.

Eva and Lora go to Chicago to meet with Mac, the renegade Councillor. He fools them into abandoning their Guardian escort, then takes them captive on his ship. They are even more shocked when Solaris appears and they discover Mac is in league with him.

While Hans' men are blinded by their own greed, Sam and Xavier make good their escape, snatching back the Gear as they flee through the perilous caves and tunnels. They have almost made it when Stella confronts them on the waterfall ledge.

Sam and Rapha take a breathtaking leap from the ledge, but it is too late—Rapha is hit by Stella's darts and passes out. Sam struggles to hold on to him as the glider twists out of control. Rapha threatens to fall from his grip as they crash towards the rocky mountain . . .

SAM

"**R**apha!" Sam screamed frantically.

Sam could see the two small darts still lodged in Rapha's back. His eyes flicked to Rapha's face—he was unconscious, his face empty.

The lush green forest that stretched out below seemed to be approaching much faster.

Just got to hold on . . .

Everything went eerily silent as they tumbled through the air towards the cliff face. Preparing himself for the impact that he knew was coming, Sam tensed his legs, straining to keep his tenuous grip on Rapha's jacket.

Calculating the timing carefully as they neared the cliff, Sam pushed hard with his legs against the vertical rock wall a split second before they would have slammed into it. The shock pulsed through his legs as he felt the glider shudder and turn sharply in the air, their trajectory changing immediately. Sam struggled and looked upward but the thick band of cloud they had plummeted through was already concealing everything.

If I can't see them, they can't see us either . . .

Sam's arm seared in agony, trying to hold on to both the makeshift glider and Rapha's deadweight. His fingers, desperately grasping the smooth metal bar above, were sweaty and slippery in the humid air of the jungle. His teeth clenched tight as he tried to keep his grip.

Suddenly, a gust of wind buffeted them from the side. Sam's fingers slid off the bar, beginning their inevitable free fall towards the imposing green below.

Sam screamed, his voice echoing out over the jungle. Still clinging to the unconscious Rapha, he stretched out his free arm, and changed his Stealth Suit into the wing-suit, clearly recalling Jedi's instructions. Their descent slowed, but with only one free arm to steer, Sam and Rapha hurtled downward, flipping and turning erratically.

CRASH!

"Argh!" Sam held his free hand over his face as they smacked through the tops of the trees. The snapping branches and vines slowed their crash-landing, but whipped into Sam's face over and over again.

THUD!

Sam landed heavily on his back and lay there silently catching his breath, staring back up into the hole they had torn through the leafy canopy above. His arm, still holding his friend, had twisted awkwardly in the rough landing. Sam could see Rapha's chest moving with slow and even breaths, and he appeared to have survived the rough landing with nothing more than a scratch or two.

"Owww . . ." Sam winced again as he tried to free his arm from underneath Rapha. "He's obviously not a light sleeper then . . ."

Through the broken branches overhead Sam could see that their crude glider was still drifting down towards the forest floor, its landing slower and more graceful now that it was without passengers. He noticed the small dents and scratches all over its surface, no doubt from the stun darts shot by Stella as they made their getaway.

A memory jolted Sam upright and he reached around to feel for his backpack. With a relieved sigh, he felt it still in place on his back, and he wriggled out of the straps and pulled it open. There, nestled safely inside, was Rapha's Gear—the priceless piece his enemies would literally kill to get their hands on in order to get one step closer to building the Bakhu machine.

Piece by piece, Gear by Gear . . . that's five down, eight to go.

"Hey," said a small voice beside him. "What did I miss?"

"Rapha!" Sam said, surprised. "Are you OK?"

"I think so," Rapha said, sitting up slowly and rubbing his head. He looked around the jungle floor and then up at the hole their descent had punched through the trees. Sam saw Rapha's eyebrows lift in surprise and the corners of his mouth curl up into a smirk.

"Maybe you should stick to being the pilot?" Sam said, following his upward gaze.

Rapha's grin spread wider, before his face suddenly

changed into a confused frown. He twisted his shoulders uncomfortably, reaching one arm behind his back and pulling the two small darts out from in between his shoulder blades. He stared at Sam, questioning.

"Oh, those . . ." Sam said sheepishly. "Sorry, I forgot they were still there. If it makes you feel any better, the darts are usually much bigger and knock you out for a lot longer."

Rapha rolled his eyes and threw the small darts into the jungle. "So what now?" he asked Sam.

"I don't suppose you have another aircraft hidden away close by?"

"No, sorry," Rapha replied. He shrugged, then said, "So we'll take a walk."

"You . . . call . . . this . . . a *walk*?" Sam stopped at a tree and shook the last drop from his water bottle. "Try hike . . . or trek . . . or a cross-jungle *marathon*."

They'd been hiking through the jungle for over an hour, sticking close to the river. Rapha had made sure they kept a quick pace, urging Sam on whenever he slowed for a drink. Despite the humid air feeling so wet against his skin, Sam had never been so thirsty.

"It's not much further," Rapha said at last. "Just up here."

"You said that an hour ago at the clearing." Sam adjusted his backpack across his shoulders.

"I thought that was another clearing," Rapha said, leading the way.

"Well, I guess, to be fair . . ." Sam said, pausing again as they came to a drop-off in the hillside, "it *is* the Amazon."

"Ha! There it is!" Rapha said, triumphantly pointing below. "That's our way out of here."

Sam saw a winding strip of water, a tributary of the Amazon River, snaking away into the distance. There wasn't much of anything else.

"And, we, ah, swim from there?" Sam asked.

Rapha smiled. "You'll see."

"I use this to map areas of the jungle and follow the migrating patterns of the geese," Rapha said cheerfully.

"Geese?" Sam asked.

"A type of bird."

"Right. Thanks."

Sam climbed into the small boat. It teetered and bobbed in the murky water and he concentrated on keeping his balance. He sat at one end and watched Rapha jump into the boat in one quick movement that barely made the boat rock.

"First you had the speedboat, then the ultralight, now this. How come?" Sam asked.

"Well, if you remember, the first speedboat was only

borrowed," Rapha corrected. "And this," he continued, "belongs to that eighty-year-old man over there."

Sam looked over to the shack standing alongside the rough jetty that serviced the local boats.

"My parents were well-known in this community. They did a lot of work for conservation and the local villages in the area . . ." Rapha's voice trailed off in sadness at the thought of his parents. Sam could see the grief fill Rapha's eyes and he looked back at the river, feeling awkward, not sure if he should try to say anything of comfort.

What could I say, anyway? I've only made things even more dangerous for him.

Rapha sighed determinedly and pulled the cord on the boat's outboard motor with a short, sharp movement. Silence. "She's a little temperamental."

A small group of locals were watching from in front of the shack, as if waiting for an invitation to lend a hand. Rapha adjusted the dials and tried again. Nothing. Sam could smell gasoline fumes in the air. He felt anxious sitting there, in clear view of everyone. He glanced around and wondered when Stella would catch up to them.

CLICK! VRROOM!

On the third try, the engine spluttered to life, almost drowning out the cheers of their small crowd of onlookers. Rapha shot Sam a confident grin, turning to wave back to the locals before steering the boat out to begin its cruise up the river.

We got Rapha's Gear, and we got away from Hans and Stella. That's a pretty good day's work.

Settling into the boat, Sam smiled at Rapha and leaned against his backpack, watching as the amazing jungle scenery drifted by.

SAM'S NIGHTMARE

The water below us is crystal clear and blue, the sand golden. Against it all, the sunlight is brilliant and glaring.

"Here they come," the girl next to me says.

Her yellow scuba vest has a flag emblazoned on it and a name written in black marker: *MARIA*.

I look in the direction she motions, wondering who "they" are. She's pointing to the water.

"Look, there are four of them," Maria says.

I see the movement below. Dark shapes slice the water. They move fast and with grace, predators at their ease.

"Are they . . ." I begin, my voice wary.

"Lemon sharks. They're like puppy dogs," Maria says, her tone matter-of-fact. She pulls on her face mask and puts her head into the sea, looking down and scanning the scene below. She emerges and says, "Come on, coast is clear."

"What?"

"Let's go." She turns her back to the edge of the little pontoon boat, and before I can object or question her, she holds a hand to her face mask to keep it in place and tips backward into the water.

"Swimming with sharks . . . great," I say, looking around. There is no one else around and no land in sight. Just this little boat in a calm, shallow sea in the middle of nowhere. I press on the regulator to check it's clear and working, then chomp down on it, put on my goggles and plunge backward over the side.

SPLASH!

I am enveloped in the warm ocean. The sounds of the underwater world around me make me feel like I'm on another planet. I hear my breathing as if I am in a space suit. It takes a while for me to get my bearings. I see Maria. She is in front of me, hand-feeding the sharks.

Slowly, cautiously, I swim over to her. The sharks don't look as big as I thought they were from above. They are about four feet long, sleek and graceful. They swish toward Maria and take chunks out of a big piece of fish she is holding. I could almost imagine them playing with her. It reminds me of playing with my beagle, Scout, back home.

That's it, just think of them as big, sweet, dopey dogs. Labradors of the sea. Nothing to be afraid of.

One flashes by me and bumps me with its tail and the regulator pops from my mouth.

Yeah, right.

I panic and grab for it, holding my breath until I reposition the mouthpiece and the sweet air mix fills my lungs once more. Maria points to a large wire basket on the seabed below us, signaling for me to get another piece of fish. I swim down, just a few kicks away and undo the latch.

Another shark bumps me away—a friendly bump, as far as I can tell. I take out a big piece of fish and refasten the basket, swimming up to be shoulder to shoulder with Maria. Hundreds of small fish, colorful and agile, dart around us as we float there, happily feeding and playing tug-of-war with the lemon sharks.

Maria pokes me in the arm, her eyes suddenly wide and pointing urgently ahead.

A huge shape appears from the dark-blue gloom in the distance. As I peer forward, wondering what the shape can be, it's upon us with a sudden surge of speed.

It's another shark. But this thing is *huge*.

We're going to need a bigger piece of fish.

I freeze, looking to Maria for a cue. She is frozen too, her eyes following the new shark warily. With a few rapid flicks of its tail, the predator flashes by us, the lemon sharks scattering in fright.

I can see the distinctive pattern along its mighty flank— it's a tiger shark. On one side of his head, a massive scar zigzags along his skin. I watch, mesmerized, as he circles us twice and then swims off, disappearing from view.

Maria points up and we swim together towards the surface.

We emerge near the boat and Maria climbs aboard in one easy move. I can see that she's spooked.

"I thought," I say, slightly out of breath as she helps pull me aboard, "that you liked sharks."

Maria shakes her head. I can see she's more than spooked, she's terrified.

"Not Scarface," she says. "He's no normal shark."

She walks around the sides of the boat, peering over, looking for him down there.

"What do you mean 'not normal?'" I ask, sitting up and shaking off my diving gear.

"He's super aggressive," Maria says. "Last summer, he knocked my friend out of the boat. He got him."

"What does that mean?"

Maria is silent as she watches the water.

"Maria—what does 'got him' mean?"

"Hold on!" she screams, grabbing on to the rope that runs through the sides of the pontoons of our boat. "Quick!"

I grab the rope at the same moment as the boat is lifted into the air. It's like there is an explosion underneath us, water erupting violently into the air as we splash down again. Maria wastes no time, moving swiftly to the controls and turning the key in the engine's ignition.

"It's not working!" she yells, running back to inspect the outboard motor. She flicks a switch. "Sam! Try it again!"

I go to the helm and turn the ignition key, but still nothing.

THUMP!

With a shudder even stronger than before, the front of the boat rises unsteadily, knocking us both to the floor. I pull myself up onto my knees, grabbing the edge of the wildly rocking boat as blood trickles from the grazes along my knuckles. The shark breaches in the water so close to the side of the boat, I could almost reach out and touch his silvery skin. I watch awestruck as he flies through the air, then splashes down headfirst. I hold my breath waiting for the next hit, but the water around us calms, lapping quietly against the sides of the boat.

"Wh . . . what . . . what do we do? Is he gone?" I ask Maria, fighting to find the words.

Maria nods. "For now." She watches the surface of the sea warily, trying to decide our next move. "Scarface is territorial. Anyone or anything is a threat to him."

"Then let's go!"

"But what we need is here," she says.

"Where?" I ask, before understanding what Maria means. "*Down there?* There was nothing there but sharks!"

"Nothing *you* saw," Maria replies, "because you weren't really looking."

"The Gear?"

Maria nods. "But Scarface is scarier than your Solarium."

"Solaris," I say, suddenly comprehending.

I've missed the start of the dream. I've already told her about the prophecy.

"His name's Solaris," I add. "And if the Gear is here, then he will be too. We have to go."

"I'll radio for help," Maria says. "Hopefully Scarface will keep anyone down there occupied."

She picks up the radio speaker, clicking the button several times.

"What is it?" I ask.

"The radio's dead." She flicks the dials but none work. "We've got no power at all."

We stare at each other and I can see the fear growing in her eyes, mirroring my own worry.

"I'll check the engine again," she says.

I stay at the controls, watching as Maria takes the cover off the outboard motor, inspecting inside.

"Maria?"

She holds up a transparent hose.

"Someone cut our fuel line," she says, her head flicking around rapidly, surveying beyond the boat. "But–we're alone . . . aren't we?"

I look around too. There's no one out here. No boats. No people. No aircraft. Nothing, as far as the eye can see.

"Maybe it snapped?" I say, joining her, looking at the fuel line, clearly cut in two. "Can you tape or stick it back together?"

She shakes her head. "Look."

Behind us is a rainbow-colored slick spreading far over the surface of the water. It smells of gasoline.

"But how . . ." I stop talking as our boat rocks unevenly again.

"Scarface!"

"No," I say, trying to stay calm. "Worse."

I instinctively flinch from the figure who is standing at the bow of the boat. Tall, in a black bodysuit, his face completely covered by a mask. Water trickles down the length of the suit, making his menacing, shimmering appearance even more ominous.

He can breathe underwater?

Solaris stands facing us, his arm raised, his flame weapon pointed and ready.

"Sam and Maria," Solaris says, his voice metallic and rasping. "Time for another swim."

"You cannot . . ." Maria begins to exclaim, taking a step forward, but I grab her arm. She turns to me, searching my face for an explanation.

"We have no choice," I whisper to her.

Solaris takes a step towards us. We move back, pressed together against the side of the boat.

"NOW!" the voice demands.

"Maria!" I whisper, pointing to the water. A large, shadowy shape glides fast through the water underneath us.

"Hold on!" I shout.

SMASH!

The shark hits the boat hard, tipping it over in one fluid motion. As we careen through the air, the engine rips away from the boat and is engulfed in a fireball flaring from Solaris' hands.

WHOOSH!

Sparks shower over the surface of the water, igniting the fuel slick like a snaking fuse. The water all around us is on fire, and I can hear metallic laughter piercing my ears, so loud and grating that it hurts.

I call out to Maria, thrashing in the waves and debris, but I can't see her through the smoke. I strike out towards the sinking boat, fearful of seeing Solaris, wondering how I will fight him in the water. I'm almost there when I feel a pull on my leg. I spin around, my heart stopping in fear. There is the flash of a sinister shadow right under me. I lash out frantically but Scarface comes for me, dragging me down to my–

Doom.

SAM

Sam snapped awake, his sudden movement tipping the boat out of its rhythm. The thick, humid air made it hard to breathe. He looked around and realized with relief where he was. He slunk back down feeling sluggish and sapped of energy.

Rapha was watching him carefully, one hand on the throttle of the boat's outboard motor. "Bad dream?"

"Something like that," Sam said, shaking his head a little and trying to make his voice even.

"We're running low on fuel but we're almost there."

Sam stood and looked at the view. A small city stretched out before them, the sun catching the tips of an endless expanse of roofs. The river was now busy with boats.

"Welcome to Rio Branco," Rapha said.

"It's big," Sam said. "I thought we were in the middle of Amazonian nowhere?"

Rapha laughed. "Lots of people live in the middle of the jungle, my friend. There is an airport here and you can fly away with your Gear."

"*Your* Gear," Sam said. "You're still a part of this, Rapha.

I need you to come along with me back to the Academy, to see out the rest of this prophecy. Can you do that?"

Rapha smiled and nodded. "I'm actually glad to hear that. I'd like to learn more about this race."

A heat haze rose from the hot tarmac of the airport, and Sam blinked away the memory of his nightmare. He had kept going over and over the details in his mind as they had traveled through the busy streets from the wharf to the airport in an old taxi.

Maria, in Cuba. She knows where the next Gear is.

Oh, and sharks. And Solaris.

Sam now paced the floor of the terminal, his backpack slung over his shoulder in readiness. He'd called Xavier and Tobias hours earlier, and they were on their way, but time seemed to be racing by while he could only keep pacing in frustration, waiting, doing nothing.

C'mon, c'mon . . . we have to get out of here before someone finds us. We have to keep moving.

Beside him, slumped in an uncomfortable chair, Rapha slept soundly with a baseball cap, newly purchased at the souvenir store, pulled down over his face.

Tobias hadn't sounded too concerned about Rapha's lack of belongings, passport or any identification. "We'll take care of it, Sam," he'd assured him.

Sam kept walking around, looking out of the big glass windows at the tourists and commuters happily heading to their next destination.

"What did you dream of?" Rapha asked out of nowhere, making Sam jump. Sam looked down at him, his face still obscured by the cap.

"Before? On the boat?"

"Yeah."

"A little bit of who the next Dreamer is—where I need to be next," Sam replied, trying to recall the details. "I find it hard, without writing it down straightaway, to remember everything. It's like I'm in this in-between world of being asleep and awake. I keep going over and over it, so I don't forget the little things, but . . ."

"So where do you have to go?" Rapha asked, his voice still sleepy.

"I don't know exactly," Sam admitted. "But I didn't know exactly where you'd be either, and look how that turned out."

Sam could see Rapha's chest moving, and it looked as if he was laughing quietly to himself under his hat. Then, from behind the row of chairs, towards the back of the terminal, Sam could see Tobias and Xavier hurrying down the busy corridor, looking at the faces of everyone as they rushed past.

"Tobias!" Sam called.

Sam saw the immediate relief on the faces of his old high school teacher and classmate at the sound of his voice. They both waved across the room.

When they reached Sam, Tobias ruffled Sam's hair in greeting and Xavier leaned forward, trying to give him a friendly pat on the back, but missing and tapping his shoulder awkwardly instead. Sam laughed.

Rapha stood up from his seat, adjusting the cap to now sit properly on his head. He held out his hand as Sam introduced him to his friends.

"Good to meet you, Rapha," said Tobias, shaking the outstretched hand. Then he added, "Well, that's the introductions done, let's get going!"

Climbing into the plane's small six-person cabin and buckling in, Sam felt relief wash over him again. His task in Brazil was over and he was with his friends once more, the Gear safely in his backpack. Looking at Tobias and Xavier climbing aboard, he reflected that it still felt odd seeing them like this. Not that long ago, Tobias had been lecturing about Newton's laws at the front of the classroom, while Xavier sat a few desks away taking notes.

Now, here we are, going from one adventure to the next, danger and death around every corner, trying to save the world . . . what a difference a month makes!

Tobias asked, "How are you?"

"Yeah, been OK," Sam said. "You know how it is."

"Ha, I sure do," Tobias said, buckling into the pilot's seat.

Wow, is there anything he can't do? And I used to think he was just a science teacher . . .

Xavier sat down beside him in the copilot's chair and started pressing buttons.

Tobias playfully smacked Xavier's hands away. "First stop, Miami," Tobias said, "and then a flight to London. There's a storm rolling around in the Gulf, from the north-east, but we should be able to skirt around it, maybe head closer to Cuba."

Sam smiled. The plane's engine started up with a loud roar and the propeller engaged. Tobias soon had them taxiing to the end of the runway, where he powered up and lifted them into the air.

Sam felt like a seasoned air traveler now. Before the last few weeks, he'd only been on a few flights, the longest one to Europe and back, and a couple of interstate trips, all family vacations. Now he'd been on long-haul flights, in helicopters and on supersonic aircraft loaded with stealth technology. Sam thought back to his recent ultralight flight over the Amazon rain forest with Rapha.

I guess I can add that to the list now.

"I'm gonna miss Brazil," Rapha said, seemingly for the millionth time since they'd arrived at the airport.

"You'll be back," Sam said, looking across the aisle to his fellow Dreamer. "Soon as all this is over, yeah?"

Rapha nodded.

"Least you've had your dream," Sam added, then looked out his window at the land below that became more and more distant and indistinct. "Mine happen every day."

"But you're still useful," Rapha replied. "I'm just along for the ride now."

"You're still useful too," Sam said, snapping out of his reverie. "All the 13 Dreamers are important, right up to the end, you'll see."

"I'll second that," Xavier said, grinning as he unbuckled and climbed through to the little cabin, passing around packages of snacks. "So, sleepyhead, you know where we're headed next?"

"Cuba," Sam replied.

"*Cuba?*" Tobias said. "Wait—you've had your next dream already?"

"I didn't tell you?" Sam teased.

"Ah, *no*," Tobias said. "And the next Dreamer?"

"A girl, Maria," Sam said. "I recognized the Cuban flag in my dream."

"A girl named Maria somewhere in Cuba . . ." Xavier repeated, nodding his head earnestly. "Great, that probably narrows it down to half their population."

"Once we plug into the dream-recording computer at the Academy, we'll see more," Sam said, then he looked at Tobias. "Unless we head straight to Cuba?"

"Hmm," Tobias said, scratching his chin.

"You know what puzzles me most?" Xavier said. "It's,

well, I mean, what if you don't dream about it again? And it's not like they're *recording* it, because you've already *had* the dream."

"They can retrieve dreams—go back in and see more," Sam said. "There can be places or names that get missed while you're dreaming."

"They can really do all that?" Rapha said, dumb struck.

"Yep," Sam said. "Sometimes. They can go back in and look around."

"That's . . ."

"Incredible?" Xavier offered. "Scary, weird? And you know what?"

"What?" Rapha said.

"*That's* not even the scariest thing about all this, or the weirdest."

"So what is?" Rapha said, looking genuinely spooked.

"Scariest? Solaris," Sam said immediately. "Weirdest is how the thirteen of us have our dreams. I mean, why us? How is it that we're dreaming about the Gears for the Bakhu machine, hundreds of years after da Vinci invented it? That's the mind-bender."

Rapha looked from Sam to Xavier, searching for more. Finally he asked, "So, what does this Bakhu machine *do?*"

EVA

"You see . . ." Mac said to Eva as he wrapped up his monologue, "you really could look at me as your creator."

Eva pushed her food around and refused to meet his eye. "I'd rather not, thank you. And here I was thinking you were just our *captor*."

"A god, if you will," Mac said, ignoring her quip.

"Or," Eva replied, "a deluded maniac who thinks he's far more powerful and important than he really is."

Mac laughed.

Eva gritted her teeth and fumed. She and Lora had been held hostage on Mac's ship for over twelve hours already.

I wish I could punch this guy in the nose . . . well, I could, but then what? Beat up all his huge security guards and take over the ship?

"Maybe," Mac said. "Maybe . . ."

Eva had just been presented with Mac's best sales pitch about why she should join him—he was behind her creation, and the creation of some of the last 13, as part of the original government-run Enterprise, who had conducted the initial research. His genetics work had led to the discovery of the Dreamer Gene, he said—the part of humanity's genetic makeup that connected people to their true dreaming abilities.

If Lora wasn't still locked up somewhere on this ridiculous yacht, I might just have seen what would happen if I did punch Mac in the nose.

"So what? So you had a hand in paving the way for my dreams, *and* my nightmares," Eva said, sitting in the plush chair opposite. "So I guess now I know who to blame." The ship had been underway through the night but she had no idea where they were, although through the window she saw the lights of a shoreline twinkle brightly.

"Blame?" Mac said, sitting back in his chair and lighting a cigar. "My dear Eva, you have been given a gift. Clearly it's beyond anything that you can imagine right now."

Eva looked at him with a tiny hint of interest.

"This race to the Dream Gate?" Mac said. "It's just the start. A small introduction to your talents. You'll continue to have your dreams, seeing events that will happen in real life, for the rest of your days."

"Wow," Eva said, full of fake amazement at the revelation. "*Everyone dreams*, what an astounding discovery."

"Not like you."

Eva looked at him. "So, what are you saying? You and Solaris want to mine my dreams forever? First to find the machine and control the world, then—then? What's after that? You'll already *have* the world."

"Solaris?" Mac said, his tone annoyed. "*He's* only interested in one thing."

"Using the Bakhu machine to find the Dream Gate?" Eva said.

"That's correct. He, like so many others, is intoxicated by its promised power. But that's such a shortsighted adventure. Lucky for you he's already left the ship to pursue his one and only goal. Me? I don't believe in fairy tales. I don't believe that this Dream Gate is anything other than an ancient myth, cooked up by Egyptian priests so that they could hang on to as much power as possible. But I *do* believe in what I *see*."

"Then take a look in a mirror sometime," Eva said, pushing her food away. "You might get a shock."

"Hmm. You have fight in you, Eva. I like that. You'd work well on my team. You know you can see the future, you told me yourself about dreaming of how you met Sam and Alex on the helicopter. Think of what you might see in the future."

"A way off this boat," Eva replied.

"Quite possibly, but you can leave whenever you like," Mac said.

"Oh, really?" Eva said, a little taken aback. "I thought Lora and I . . ."

"I mean it—you are free to go whenever you like," Mac said.

Eva stared pointedly at the two men standing guard just inside the doorway.

"Yes, yes, I have security, of course I do," Mac dismissed their presence with the wave of a hand. "But I just want you to hear what I have to say, so that you may understand where I am coming from. This is a matter of more than just life and death for me or you."

"OK . . ." Eva said, leaning back in her chair. "Go on."

"Eva, I believe you will become a very powerful Dreamer indeed. You will see wars before they are fought. You will see the changes in world economies and politics long before they occur. You will be able to discover unknowns before anyone else . . . you, Eva, are our *future*."

"Yeah, like I said before, *wow*," Eva said, nonplussed. "I'm a Dreamer. I get that. All I care about is my friends, this race to the Dream Gate and making sure that we win."

"Win?" Mac scoffed.

"That's right. That we get there first. That we beat everyone else—you, Solaris, Stella, Hans, whoever—whoever wants to get to the Dream Gate and use it for evil."

"Evil?" Mac repeated again. "We're all a little bit evil somewhere inside ourselves."

"Not me," Eva said decidedly.

"You have no idea, do you?" Mac said to her. "You're not just any Dreamer, Eva."

Eva battled with wanting to know what he was getting at but not wanting to give him the satisfaction of having her intrigued.

"That's what I'm trying to tell you here," Mac said, the expression on his face almost becoming friendly. "You're so much more than that. So much more . . ."

"I know, I get it. You think that I'm one of the 13," Eva said, exasperated. "You're wasting your time here."

"We'll see," he said. "I bet I can change your mind."

SAM

"OK . . ." Rapha said, having listened to Sam, Xavier and Tobias all explain the Gears, the Bakhu machine and the Dreamer lore about the last 13. "So, we are joined to this race through our dreams—like destiny."

"Destiny," Sam said, "and some of the 13 are enhanced at a DNA level, sharing genetic information that goes back to some of the greatest Dreamers in history, like da Vinci and Archimedes and Aristotle."

"A Dreamer Gene," Tobias added. "Some have it in their natural makeup, while others of the 13 had a little genetic help in their creation."

"Wow," Rapha said. "That's crazy."

Sam nodded but Xavier shook his head.

"Well," Xavier said, "for me, what really blows *my* mind and freaks *my* bones, is this whole da Vinci thing."

"Da Vinci thing?" Rapha said.

"Long story," Sam said, sitting back in the airplane seat and trying to relax.

"Create us, enhance us, whatever, to have vivid dreams," Xavier said, "then train us to master our dreams and use the dream world to alter the reality that later pans out. OK, that's plausible."

Sam rolled his eyes, knowing where this was going.

"But each of us having a dream that leads to a Gear to build a machine that da Vinci made, like, *over five hundred years ago?*" Xavier went on. "Gears that are scattered *all* around the world, lost in time? To find a Dream Gate that is thousands of years old? Yeah, *that's* the mind-blowing stuff right there."

Rapha looked at the brass Gear in his hands.

"Yeah," Sam said. "But it hurts my mind just trying to think about that."

"So just go with it?" Xavier said.

"What else can we do?" Sam asked. "They've explained it to us at the Academy, but the rest is up to us. It *is* happening, so we know it's real. I think we have to accept that there are things going on here that defy logic. But the world moves in mysterious ways, as do dreams. The mind, the collective consciousness, the dreams—all of it is true, we've seen that. It . . . it is what it is, and it makes . . . not *sense*, but it's believable."

"With every day," Tobias added, "it becomes more believable."

Rapha nodded but Xavier looked unconvinced. His dream had led them to the Gear in Berlin, but Solaris had taken it from them.

Maybe that's it. Xavier found his Gear but we lost it.

Maybe that's what's making him so skeptical now?

"I believe it, Sam," Xavier said, "like I believe in gravity, like I believe in all the science I know to be true, like Newton's laws of physics. But I just want to understand *how* it all works."

Sam nodded. This was the Xavier he'd known at school—always questioning, always wanting to know every little detail about everything. His father, Dr. Dark, was a brilliant psychiatrist and Dreamer, with the same inquisitive nature about the world and everyone in it.

So Xavier will probably always be like this, like his father—it's a Dark family trait.

"To me, the 'how' is not that important," Sam said, and Xavier shook his head. "I don't want to overanalyze it—at least not right now. Afterwards? Sure, I'll study the legs off it."

Xavier laughed.

"Until then," Sam went on, "I *trust* it, rather than question it."

"As a scientist," Tobias said, "I look at it as a new frontier, some kind of new science—somewhere between physics and psychology and noetics and whatever else."

"No-what?" Rapha asked.

"Don't ask," Sam said.

"Seriously!" Xavier added. "Don't get him started on his pet science topic."

"Guys, I'm hurt," Tobias said with a laugh.

"You mean as Dreamers we are like discoverers, or explorers," Rapha said, his gaze far-off as it sunk in.

"Exactly!" Sam said. "And these Gears are part of a machine, a device that will lead us to the Dream Gate. Think of it as the world's first GPS."

Rapha held up the Gear to catch the light. The brass was green in places, where it had been exposed to the air for too long in the hidden Amazonian city.

Rapha nodded. Xavier did too.

"That all sounds great," Xavier said, "but that's only if there will *be* a 'later' when we can ask all those questions and study it. I mean, you're assuming that we win."

"We won't lose this race," Sam said, his jaw clenched in determination. "We can't."

ALEX

Alex sat in the Professor's office at the Academy, along with the director of the Enterprise, Jack, his mother, Phoebe, and two of the last 13, Zara and Gabriella. It felt weird being there—so much had changed since he had met the Professor at the Academy's now-destroyed Swiss campus.

At first Alex had been surprised at the friendliness between the Professor and the director. He'd once assumed, from his first encounter with the Enterprise when their Agents kidnapped him, that all they were interested in was winning at any cost.

Even if that meant lives lost along the way.

Like Sebastian in New York.

But not anymore. Now, he better understood the Enterprise's motives. They did not want the Dream Gate to end up in the hands of evil any more than the Academy did. And now that Stella was controlling a rogue group of Agents and working with Solaris, the Academy and the Enterprise had no choice but to work together. The Professor clearly understood this, and so did Jack. Without each other's help and knowledge, there was no hope on the path ahead.

So from here on in, we're all in this together.

And for the last few minutes, they'd been discussing the latest efforts to locate and rescue their missing friends, Lora and Eva.

"Can't we just have the navy or someone hunt down Mac's boat?" Alex asked.

"Mac has powerful friends," Jack said. "The Guardians who were watching over them in a helicopter were forced to land by the local police who didn't realize what was happening. By the time it got straightened out and they got back in the air, Mac's boat had slipped away."

"It's not registered anywhere, so I'm afraid we can't track it," the Professor added.

"I promise you—we're working on it," Jack said. "We'll catch up with Mac soon."

"It's my fault," the Professor said, his voice grave. "I should never have allowed that meeting—I should have overruled Lora."

"But we all know that's not your style," Jack replied. "Besides, Lora being overruled? Please. You'd have better luck convincing her that the world was flat."

"It isn't?" Alex said.

The Professor chuckled. "And what about the Gears?" he asked, letting out a sigh as he conceded everything was being done to find Lora and Eva.

"Here's what we know for sure," the director said, opening up his laptop. With a few clicks, he projected a huge map of the world on the wall of the Professor's office. "So far we have recovered the pieces to the Bakhu machine from New York, Italy, Germany, France and now Brazil."

"And of those," the Professor said, pointing to Gabriella's Gear and Sam's key locked in a secure glass-fronted vault set into his wall, "only those found in New York, Italy and Brazil remain in our possession."

"Correct." The director tapped away at his laptop and the wall screen was updated with more information. "Solaris has the Gears found in Germany and France, and his last known sighting was in Paris."

"By Sam and Zara?" the Professor said.

"That's also correct."

"I wish I had, how do you say, punched?" Zara looked to Gabriella, who nodded, understanding exactly how she felt. "Yes, I wish I punched Solaris across his face. Smashed that stupid mask."

"You'll get your chance," Phoebe said with a grimace.

"And what of our other threats?" the Professor asked.

"Hans is on the move and was last seen here, at the site in Brazil," the director said, bringing up a dot marker that flashed red on the eastern border of Brazil. "Our contacts in German customs reported that his aircraft returned this morning to Berlin, but there were no passengers."

"And we don't know where he is?" the Professor asked.

"No," the director said. "But I have Agents at every major airport throughout North and South America, working alongside your friends in the Dreamer Council and their local law enforcement connections."

"Looking out for him and his entourage of German Guardians?" the Professor said, and the director nodded. "I fear that with his wealth and power, he'll find a way to slip away."

"We are doing our best," the director replied tersely.

"Why did they turn?" Alex asked.

"We're working on figuring that out," the Professor replied. "But there are factions running right through our Dreamer Council and now Mac's supporters have left us."

"Which brings us back to our pressing issue—Mac," the director said.

"He'll be planning his next move, that is certain," the Professor replied. "And he is more dangerous to us than ever, now that he has Eva and Lora to bargain with."

"So what about Stella?" Alex asked.

He could see that it pained the director that his trusted operations leader, Stella, had gone to the other side of the race to the Dream Gate. Of all their growing list of enemies, she was the only one they knew for sure was working with Solaris. Alex had overheard her plotting with him in Berlin.

"Stella, I'm happy to say, we have a bit more on," the director said. "She was last seen by Sam, and the latest Dreamer, Rapha, at the Gear site in Brazil, where she and her men became locked in a battle with Hans' Guardians."

"Well, at least that tells us that they're not working together," Phoebe said.

"My thoughts exactly," the Professor added.

"That's right," the director said, then brought up a location marker in Canada. "Stella was spotted here, less than an *hour* ago."

"That's near Vancouver, isn't it?" Phoebe said.

"Yes."

"What's there?" Gabriella asked. "A Gear?"

"I don't think so," the Professor replied, deep in thought. "When Tobias called from Rio Branco airport he made no mention of Sam's next dream."

"Can we have local authorities arrest her?" Zara asked.

"She'll have already vanished into the ether," the director said. "But we have assets moving to the scene, to track her on the ground."

"Can you think of any reason she would be in Vancouver?

Do you have anything there?" the Professor asked. "Any secret locations there that your Agents use?"

"No, our Canadian sites are in Toronto and Montreal."

"Then why is she there?" Alex asked.

"I have no idea . . ." the director's voice trailed off and he stood, stunned, staring at the projection on the wall. A list of archived events from the Vancouver area was displayed on the screen.

"What is it?" Alex asked.

"Oh no . . ." the director said, looking to them all in the room, his expression a mix of shock and realization. "There is an old site, from the government program that closed down years ago . . ."

"What's the site used for now?" the Professor asked.

"Nothing, it was abandoned," the director replied, reading off the data. "It's buried deep underground, it was a part of a Cold War military base, a command backup center in the event of an all-out war."

"But the facility is still there?"

"Yes." The director hurriedly dialed a number on his mobile phone. "And if we hurry, maybe we can catch her there."

"Jack," the Professor said. "This site—what was it used for?"

The director looked to Phoebe then shook his head. "You don't want to know."

SAM

"**W**e're going to have to detour around this weather system and hunker down," Tobias called into the cabin of the plane. They'd been flying for a couple of hours, and now he and Rapha were wrestling with the controls as they struggled against the storm ahead of them. "I've just gotten clearance to land in Cuba."

"Stay the night in Cuba?" Sam said. He immediately thought of Maria.

But could I really find her, with what little I have from my dream?

"Yep," Tobias replied, then went silent as he concentrated on landing in the dark, wet world that surrounded them. The lights of a tiny runway glittered far below.

Sam nodded. Rapha, for all his flying experience in his ultralight, looked a motion-sickness shade of green.

"You OK?" Sam asked him, the little plane jinking and bucking in the storm.

Rapha nodded. "Sure."

"You know, this could be worse," Sam called over the sound of the ferocious storm. The world seemed to grow more sinister with every foot they descended towards their landing site in Cuba.

"How do you figure that?" Tobias yelled over his shoulder, his voice shaky as the vibrations worked their way through the control yoke up his arms and through his body.

"There could be lightning," Sam said.

A flash of blinding white light pulsed outside, followed instantly by the loud rumble of thunder.

"That was—"

There was another flash, instantly accompanied by more thunder, as if tearing the sky to pieces.

"Close!" Tobias finished. He fell silent as he wrestled against the elements to guide them down to safety.

Rapha looked over his shoulder to Sam, and neither of them spoke again as Tobias brought the aircraft in to land.

They could have been anywhere in the world—the torrential rain was an impenetrable curtain that made it impossible to see across the city street. The only thing that made Sam aware that he was in a city unlike any he'd been to before was the taxi they were riding in. The beautiful clunker was at least sixty years old and sounded as though it were powered by a tractor engine.

No, scrap that—tractor engines are quieter.

Their hotel was a building by the port and the four of them sat inside a suite, watching the stormy night through the open balcony doors. It was humid and still pouring outside. It was possible to make out some of the landscape across the marina when the sky was momentarily lit up by flashes of bright lightning.

"Cuba's one of the few countries in the world where we don't have Guardians," Tobias said, sipping his coffee. "So we'd better not leave the hotel unless in a group."

"Sure," Xavier replied.

"Is that why you weren't sure if we should travel straight here?" Sam asked.

"Partly," Tobias nodded.

But Sam was more confident. He was glad that the weather had changed their plans. Since landing, he'd had that familiar sense of déjà vu, along with the kind of anticipation that came with waking early on Christmas morning or on his birthday, thinking about the excitement the day would bring. Sam knew by now that this feeling always followed closely after he had a dream. Maria was here, in Cuba, he knew it and he could *sense* it.

"Sam, you OK?" Tobias said.

"Ah, yeah, sure," Sam replied. "Just tired."

Tobias paused and said, "Thinking about Maria?"

Sam nodded.

"We'll find her, but not in this weather, and not with the little you can recall from your dream. Hang tight, yeah?"

Sam nodded again.

I want to be sure before I say anything. Take it carefully.

There was a knock at the door and Rapha went to open it. He came back, wheeling a trolley from room service. Sam plugged in his huge brick of a phone to charge. The special handset that Jedi had given him looked a little worse for wear, covered in mud and scratches from his time in Brazil.

"Food's up!" Xavier called, helping himself to the plates on the trolley. "Oh man, I'm starving!"

"Help yourself, Rapha," Tobias said. "I ordered two of everything from the menu."

"Yeah, there's enough here to feed an army," Xavier said, taking a rice dish.

"Or," Rapha said, selecting a chicken burrito, "three growing boys."

"And one old man," Sam said with a grin and launched into a taco.

Tobias just smiled and took the comment in his stride.

"I've got a feeling," Sam said, adding hot sauce and sliced jalapeños, "that tonight is going to be a good night for dreaming."

"And," Xavier added, "a bad night for gas."

Sam was right.

That night, in a small bed by a half-open window with the storm raging outside, Sam *did* dream.

It was a vivid dream. But it was definitely not a good dream.

Solaris had been firing at him and Maria on the boat just as before, the leaky gasoline from the engine igniting all around him.

Now, Sam was sweaty and shaking as he sat on the edge of the bed looking out at the dark sky. The breeze was cool on his face. The rain still fell but it was lighter now. A mist of steam had rolled into the bay. He closed his eyes as the better moments of the dream flashed back as fragmented memories.

The dream was good *and* bad.

Good because he now knew where Maria was.

Funny, how things intersect between the dream world and the real world. It's as though destiny is bringing me to exactly the right place . . .

The bad part was the realization of what would happen next.

Solaris.

Did Solaris break into my dream? Or am I making him appear in my dreams? It felt like the scenery disappeared, as if he turned the Dreamscape to darkness.

Sam closed his eyes and could clearly see that dark figure that haunted his dreaming and waking life. He had said something, in that deep and evil metallic voice.

What did he say to me?

Sam looked across to the other bed in the room, where Rapha was quietly sleeping.

"I need you, Sam—and you need me. We're two parts of the same thing. The world, this race, cannot exist with just one of us. We're the same, you and I. It doesn't need to be a struggle, think of all the innocent people you could save from harm. Join me, Sam. Let's fulfill our destiny together . . ."

Sam strained to recall where they'd been at the end of his dream, but it seemed featureless, a lonely place, perhaps a desert. It was just him and Solaris. He'd forced himself awake at that point, shutting down the dream, refusing to allow Solaris to influence his sleeping mind.

Is that what they mean about steering your dream?

Now, here he sat, waiting for daybreak and fighting off fatigue, dreading returning to the dream world that beckoned if he placed his head back down upon the pillow. He checked his watch—nearly 5 a.m.

Sam put on his Stealth Suit. It was comfortable, the memory fabric forming around his body and perfectly regulating his temperature. That wasn't even its best feature—it was able to change its appearance *and* composition at the will of the user. In just the last few weeks, it had been everything from a tuxedo, to a cop's uniform to a flying wing-suit. As he caught sight of himself in the mirror, it resembled black wet-weather gear, perfect for what he wanted to do.

Pausing at the small hallway table, he wrote a note for his friends, telling them he needed some fresh air, and slipped out into the corridor.

EVA

Tap, tap, tap . . . tap, tap, tap . . .

Eva stood up and put her ear to the wall. The sound disappeared. Maybe it was something out in the water bumping against the yacht, a piece of the floating garbage that seemed to clog the waterways everywhere. She tried her door again but it was locked tight. She wanted to learn more from Mac, hoping to find some weakness to exploit, but one of his underlings had come in with an urgent call and she'd been taken back to her locked room.

Tap, tap, tap.

It's coming from the wall?

Eva tapped back, then the other tapping became a little more frantic.

"It must be Lora," Eva said to herself.

Is her room next door or further down?

Eva knew her door was locked tight. It was a small room with a double bunk—obviously part of the crew quarters and a stark contrast to the luxuries she'd seen above deck. On the other side of the room was a little porthole, barely big enough for her to put her head through.

Eva ran over, pushed the porthole open and popped her head out.

"Eva!" Lora said. Her head was sticking out the open porthole of the room next door.

"Lora!"

"Are you OK?"

"Fine. You?"

"Yes. Did they take you from your room before?"

"They did, I had a little chat with Mac." Eva squinted against the sea spray that washed over her. The portholes were close to the waterline, the green water lapping just below them. "He thinks it might be a good idea if I joined him."

"Yeah, right. Did you see Solaris?"

"No. I think he must have left last night."

Lora nodded.

"So, how do we get out of here?" Eva asked.

"We wait," Lora replied, "for an opportunity."

They looked around. There was land visible from their side of the ship but no towns or buildings of any kind.

"Where do you think we are?" Eva asked.

"Still in the lakes," Lora replied. "And we're headed west. He's keeping us moving so we're harder to track."

Eva spied a few other boats, but none of them close. She wondered if perhaps they could flag one down if it neared, somehow get word out on where they were.

"What do you think he'll do with us?"

"I think he'll do exactly what he said last night," Lora replied.

Eva thought back. They'd gone to Chicago to meet with Mac and see about his motives and, as Lora had said, *to see if he can be reasoned with.*

They'd gone to see if Mac would join them, and instead he'd asked them to join *him*. And Solaris.

"Do you think the Professor will do a trade?" Eva asked.

"No."

Eva was a little shocked.

"Not for what Mac is asking—trading Sam for us. But there's more to bargain with."

"More?" Eva asked.

"Perhaps a Gear would be enough," Lora said, staring off to the water that slipped by.

"But we've worked so hard to get those that we have . . ."

"I know," Lora said. "But we can get them back, so long as there's time. What's more important right now is you—I shouldn't have put you in danger like this. I'm so sorry."

"Please, don't. I wanted to come. If I'm not part of this fight, the race, then I don't have anything in my life anymore," Eva said. "I don't want to be sitting around while the fate of the world is decided. Besides," she smiled, "at least I'm not on my own. Don't forget that you're stuck here too."

Lora smiled. "I can take care of myself. Meantime, it's time to rest and be prepared, as soon as the slightest opportunity arises, we move—and we move fast."

SAM

The streets had been washed clean by the storm, and the air was cooler than it had been the day before. Sam guessed the heat would return after sunrise, the wet ground and dense air turning this place into a greenhouse of humidity.

As he walked the streets, he watched and listened to the town slowly waking up. Lights came on in the windows of the tiny pastel-colored houses. He heard the rattle of morning dishes as breakfasts were prepared. They were in Cienfuegos, a small city on the southern coast of Cuba, their hotel near a white sandy beach where waves slowly met the shore.

The marina must be along there somewhere.

Sam scanned the skyline and found a high point—a tall bell tower in the center of the old part of town.

That's the view I need.

He slipped from the street into the shadows of the buildings, hiding in the darkness that had yet to catch the morning light. He paused and looked around. Sam couldn't shake off the thought of Solaris. He felt as though he was being watched as he made for the bell tower.

There was a man standing next to a horse and cart on the cobbled street, delivering milk. Further away, a couple of fishermen walked up an empty alley and a few guys in the back of an old diesel truck drove past, heading to work.

"Papers."

The deep voice made Sam jump. Next to him, a tall, lean man stepped out from the shadows.

Sam was relieved.

A police officer.

"Papers," the officer repeated. His hand was outstretched to Sam.

"Ah, I left them back at my hotel," Sam replied, thinking of his passport in the backpack in his room.

The policeman eyed Sam suspiciously. "Which hotel?"

"Hotel La Union," Sam replied.

The policeman rested his hands on his hips, looking at Sam as if deciding whether to take him to the hotel to look at his papers or to just let him go.

"How old are you?"

"Fifteen," Sam replied.

"What are you doing in the streets so early?"

"Just walking."

"Walking?"

"Si," Sam said, using one of the few Spanish words he knew.

"It is dangerous to walk alone when still dark," the

policeman said, looking around. "You have family here?"

"Ah, my uncle," Sam said quickly, thinking of Tobias. "I should get back to my hotel, right?"

The policeman looked at him, his face impassive.

Sam felt even more uneasy. The street around them was still and quiet.

The policeman's gaze became cloudy, his eyes fixed in a distant stare.

"Sir?" Sam said, now worried.

Am I in trouble? Do I run?

The man suddenly slumped forward and Sam stumbled to catch him just in time, lowering him to the ground awkwardly. A dart protruded from the middle of his back.

Sam looked up.

A few paces away stood four men armed with dart guns.

Run!

ALEX

The room had been full of a tense silence since the director had explained that the Vancouver facility was the central location of the original Dreamer DNA research. Phoebe was refusing to look Alex in the eye. For his part, he tapped away at his phone, sending details of the site to Shiva. Gabriella and Zara, neither of them Enterprise-created Dreamers, sat quietly, not fully comprehending the implications of what had been said.

"I've got a security team en route, two hours out," the director said abruptly. "If they find Stella there, they'll apprehend her immediately."

Alex stood up to walk over to the large projected image and studied the diagram of the abandoned complex.

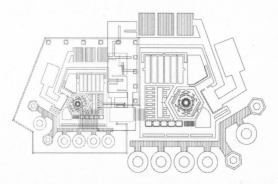

"So why do you think Stella is going there?" Alex asked.

"There's a lot of stored data within the complex, especially in the vault," the director said. "But I can't really believe that's what she's after."

The Professor came around his desk and stood next to Alex, gazing at the projection. "There are many parts to the puzzle, to this race. We need to piece them together, use all the information and knowledge we have." He turned to the director. "Jack, can you really think of nothing else there that might be useful in the race? Anything related to the Bakhu machine, the Dreamscape or da Vinci's work?"

The director paced the room as he thought out loud. "Apart from the data, there was a collection of Dreamer artifacts. Dreamer inventions and machines . . ." He gazed into space, lost for a moment.

"Jack?"

"Sir?"

"I've just realized—the code book is there. Surely that can't be it?"

"What was the book for?" the Professor asked.

"It was a guide, theoretical of course, to using Tesla's towers. We discounted it as outdated technology, focused on our genetics work. But it's possible Stella believes she and Solaris will be able to manipulate the Dreamscape with the towers, which would give them a huge advantage."

The Professor looked grave. "We found a sketch of a Tesla tower in the journal Dr. Kader sent to Sam in Brazil."

"We gotta get out there!" Alex said.

"Agreed. We must leave immediately to meet them there. Who knows, maybe there is even a Gear . . . it's possible that one could have been unknowingly gathered up in the Dreamer collection."

"If there's a chance that a Gear is at the site," Phoebe said, "we should have one of the last 13 on hand in case that helps us find it."

"I don't understand, why would we need one of the last 13 to go?" Alex asked his mother.

She looked to the director and the Professor, both of them hesitating. Finally the Professor nodded and the director turned to Alex. "These Gears," he said, "each needs one of the last 13 Dreamers to find it."

"Right . . ." Alex said.

"We also know the last 13 are somehow 'activated' by having a dream of their Gear, the Gear only they can find. I think you know that much already too."

Alex nodded. Zara and Gabriella listened with eager faces.

"Since you have been here, and in your time at the Enterprise, we have been monitoring your dreams each night," the Professor said, "as we do for all of you. And we have found a change in your sleep rhythms."

"Huh?" Alex said.

"When Gabriella, Xavier and Zara came to the Academy, we spotted the same dramatic change in their dream waves. We realized it was a distinct pattern. At first we thought it was due to the last 13 Dreamers being linked to each *other*," the Professor added. "But then we went back and saw that it had happened when Sam returned with the Star of Egypt."

"Right . . ." Alex said. "I'm with you so far, I think."

"Put simply, when one of the last 13 are physically near a *Gear*, their dream waves become altered," the Professor went on. "The connection is via the Dreamscape. The Dreamer must be aware, on a subconscious level, that the Gear is close by."

"So you're saying they're affected by being close to Sam's key and Gabriella's Gear?" Alex said.

"Indeed. We have also noticed that each of the Gears bears a specific number. Gabriella's Gear is marked with the Roman numerals for the number twelve and from the recording of Xavier's Gear dream, we were able to see the numerals for eleven." A close-up of Xavier's Gear flashed onto the screen.

"Wow," Alex said. "So how does that relate to Dreamers and the Gear proximity thing?"

"We know that da Vinci's Bakhu machine has thirteen Gears, and that they need to be put together in a specific order. But we now think that not only are the last 13 connected to their own Gear, but they also remain connected, in some lesser way, to the machine as a whole—to *all* of the Gears," the director said.

"But how?" Gabriella asked.

"Through your dream waves," the Professor answered. "Since we've had a Gear on-site, we have noticed a change in the dream patterns of *all* of the last 13 Dreamers."

"So you need Zara or Gabriella to go to Vancouver? Just in case they make it easier to find the exact location if a Gear is there?" Alex asked, finally understanding where this was going.

"Or *you*," the Professor replied, watching Alex carefully.

"M . . . me?" Alex looked from the Professor to Phoebe and back again.

"Your dream rhythms, Alex," the director said, "have all the hallmarks of one of the last 13."

"So—so I'm one of them?"

Gabriella and Zara began to smile.

"It's certainly looking that way," the Professor said.

"How do you feel about that? I know it's a big thing to take in," the director added carefully.

"I—I don't know," Alex stammered. "All this time I

wanted to be part of the race, *hoped* I would be." He looked back to his mother and saw her face creased with worry. "I know it's dangerous but it feels like it was always meant to be this way."

Now I know where I fit in.

"What about—is anyone else here also one of the last 13?" he asked, with one particular person very much in mind.

"Not conclusively. We'd prefer not to stretch the theory too far at this stage," the director said. "For now we need to focus on the mission ahead of us," he added, quickly changing the subject.

"I'm happy to go to Vancouver, if that's what you're asking," Alex said, his face resolute. His mother was silent, her face unreadable. He avoided her eyes.

"You're very perceptive, Alex," the Professor said. "Jack was hoping that you might agree to that. I have to admit that Gabriella is not yet fully recovered from her injuries and we would prefer to let Zara spend time acclimatizing to her new life here before going back out in the field."

Both Gabriella and Zara looked like they were going to protest, but a look from the Professor silenced them. Gabriella muttered something under her breath but nodded.

"I understand, it makes sense," Alex said. "Plus, I know Stella better—well, know better what she's capable of."

"I think Alex is right," the director said to Phoebe. "He's our best option."

Alex could see that the Professor still looked a little concerned. "My worry," he said, "is that if our theory about being connected to all the Gears proves false, if it *does* turn out there is another explanation, then we will have placed Alex in peril unnecessarily."

"I understand your concern," Phoebe said, finally rejoining the conversation, "but where *is* safe these days? Both the Academy and the Enterprise have suffered direct attacks, and even you personally, Professor."

"And what if I can locate a Gear?" Alex said, and he went over to the glass-fronted case, looking in at the brass-toothed Gear. "Think what an advantage that would be in the race."

"I have to say that I agree with Alex this time . . ." Phoebe said.

"Thanks, Mom," Alex said, turning around, surprised, and smiling at her.

"I wonder," Phoebe added, "if I might join my son on the mission to Vancouver, just for extra protection? It could also serve as an added cover. If others see Alex is there, they may well assume it's because he's traveling with me."

"Certainly," the Professor said, sounding reassured.

"We'll have our best Agents protecting you both," the director added. "I've learned my lesson the hard way—never again will we underestimate our enemies."

SAM

Sam hurdled over a fruit stall being set up for the day's trade and skidded over the cobbled street and down an alley. Behind, the four men were in hot pursuit.

Are they Agents? Where are their suits?

At the sound of a loud commotion, he turned and glanced behind him, turning in time to see one of the men slide and fall, clipping the side of the fruit display while attempting to make the sharp turn. The man clutched his ankle in pain as fruit and vegetables cascaded over the sidewalk and onto the street.

Ha! One down, three to go . . .

Sam turned back in time to see an approaching delivery truck with an oversized load of wood coming way too fast down the narrow alley. He ducked into a gap between two tall apartment buildings that was so narrow he had to squeeze through sideways. He was just in time to avoid being hit as the truck squeezed by.

BEEP! BEEEEP!

Sam kept running and smiled at the sound of the truck's horn blaring and the brakes squealing. The men yelled in anger at the truck driver in the alley—they had obviously been forced to back up to let the truck past.

That will buy me some time.

Sam ran on, weaving through the maze-like cobbled streets of the old part of town until he burst into the central square of a large plaza. Running to the edges and ducking into the shadows of a colonnade, he paused to catch his breath for a moment, doubled over and panting. The men were still after him, but luckily Sam was able to keep a good distance and they remained behind.

A week ago I could have run all morning, Sam thought, sucking for air. *I'm fast—but I've spent too much time on the run without resting.*

Sam knew he didn't have the energy to run these guys all over town. He decided to change tactics and find someplace to hide. Sam turned as he heard his pursuers emerge onto the far side of the plaza.

They might be slower, but they're armed and well trained. I won't get rid of them that easily.

Sam crept through the shadows, scanning all the buildings he passed but they were all little cafes and stores that were probably at least another hour away from opening. Even the church with the tall bell tower he'd seen from across town was closed. He sunk further into the shadows as the voices of the men echoed across the plaza. He saw them split up—they'd go systematically around the square, checking the buildings' fronts and would find him in less than a minute.

Where can I go?

Sam glanced around as he crept forward. He kept close to the wall behind him, staying in the gloom and skirting around the sides of the buildings.

A solution!

Sam crossed a walkway to where a ladder stretched up to a tile roof. He climbed up, then scrabbled to the top of the roof on his hands and knees.

"There!" one of the men called out behind him. They were at the base of the ladder in no time, one of them starting to climb. Sam heaved the ladder away from the building, leveraging himself against the roof, sending the leader sprawling to the ground below.

PING! PING!

Darts began to hit the guttering and roof around Sam. He kicked out at the stacks of new tiles waiting to be laid, sending a mess of broken terracotta cascading around the men below. They were forced to retreat momentarily. Sam ran agilely up the roof, across the ridge and leaped down onto the next roof.

Ahead, in the breaking dawn, Sam saw that the roofs of the old quarter of town were all the same—covered in old tiles, their similar heights and slopes marking out a terracotta path ahead.

This place was custom-made for my escape!

Sam felt a surge of energy as he ran along the roofs,

sticking to the tile ridgelines, taking twists and turns until he was brought to a sudden halt, his arms flailing back so the forward momentum did not carry him over the steep drop.

A street cut through his rooftop runway, separating him from the next building. The drop was two stories. Beyond the next row of apartments was the beachside road that he'd taken from the hotel.

He looked back where he had come from. The men were following fast along the rooftops, now only a building away from where he stood.

Twenty seconds, tops . . .

Sam contemplated the option in front of him.

No way can I make the jump to the other side. My Stealth Suit can't glide me over, there's not enough of a drop to . . . hang on, my Stealth Suit!

Sam remembered Tobias briefing him on the upgraded suit he now wore. There were more special features—one in particular that would be very handy right about now.

He changed the suit to blend into his surroundings, concentrating hard on the pattern and color of the terracotta tiles and pulling the material over himself to cover his head and hands. He was now partially invisible.

Thank you, Enterprise tech-heads.

He saw the two men stop as he disappeared. Sam knew it would only buy him a few minutes at best—as soon as he moved fast, the Stealth Suit, or more specifically his mind control, would struggle to match a rapidly moving background.

But as Sam watched, the men put on glasses, the lenses tinted light-blue and it seemed as though they could see him as clearly as before. They continued to approach, more slowly now, realizing Sam was trapped.

Uh-oh.

Two choices—drop down to the street and hope I don't break a leg, or jump and hope I make it across to the next roof . . . and don't break a leg.

The sound of running footsteps could be heard in the street below as the large guy who'd tripped over the fruit stall caught up to them. Sam could see him looking in the doorways and windows of houses in the street.

Jump, it is then.

Sam started rocking on his heels, forward and back, trying his best to convince himself he could make it, then he launched forward, flying through the air. His arms and legs flailed in midair and it felt like his world was in slow motion.

I'm gonna make it, I'm gonna make . . .

THUD!

12

EVA

The helicopter landed on another huge boat, its rotor blades whining to a slow stop. Eva could see this one was definitely no pleasure craft. Instead, it looked like an old freighter, the main deck cleared to create a makeshift helipad. Mac's security guys began to file out immediately.

"Wonder how far we've traveled?" Eva asked Lora. They'd been in the helicopter for hours. She stretched her aching legs out in front of her as one of their guards nudged them towards the door.

"OK, OK, I'm going," Eva muttered. Eva cast her eyes around the deck as she got out, but Mac was nowhere to be seen. He had departed the yacht in his own helicopter about half an hour before they were bundled into theirs.

"It's a long way to shore," Lora said out the corner of her mouth.

Eva nodded. "Take me an hour to swim that far," she said quietly. "Where do you think we are?"

"I think we're on the west coast—near Seattle," Lora said, looking towards the horizon. "Maybe even as far north as Vancouver."

"Really?" Eva craned to see in all directions but the landscape looked unfamiliar.

If we're back in my home town, it's a part of town I never saw.

Their helicopter lifted off after taking on fuel, and almost instantly another came in to land, the wind kicked up by its rotors making Eva and Lora duck for cover. Eva, squinting against the wind and dust, watched as a short woman with wiry hair and round black glasses got out.

"I don't believe it!" Eva gasped, transfixed as the woman walked towards the doors on the other side of the ship.

"What is it?" Lora asked. She looked at Eva and saw the recognition in her face. "You *know* this person?"

Eva nodded. "I do. That's my aunt."

"Your *aunt*?"

"Uh-huh. And she doesn't exactly look like she's been brought here against her will."

Lora and Eva watched as the new arrival stepped into the main cabin at the back of the ship and a moment later they were ushered there too.

As they went inside, Eva saw that what looked like a dilapidated old freighter covered in rust and mismatched paint on the outside, was in fact a state-of-the-art ship on the inside.

Is nothing what it seems anymore?

Mac was waiting for them within. "Ah, we're all here," he said, his ruddy cheeks and well-tailored clothes giving him a much more welcoming appearance than he deserved. Eva reminded herself he was a traitor and a kidnapper.

"Eva, *darling*," the woman said, walking towards her. "So nice to see you again."

"I wish I could say the same, *Aunt* Julia," Eva replied.

Julia's facial expression turned from friendly to hurt in a heartbeat. "Now, hold on a minute—" she began.

"Don't you *dare* lecture me!" Eva spat out. "Mac's a kidnapper. And now I find out my aunt is his accomplice. Not that you even *are* my aunt!"

Julia flashed a dark look at Mac, who merely shrugged.

"What can I say?" Mac said. "They needed some persuasion to stay a little longer."

Julia looked back at Eva and came up close to her. Eva was a little put off—she swore that there was concern showing in Julia's eyes.

"I *am* your aunt," Julia said. "Always have been, and always will be. My sister is your mother—and she misses you," she said. "Your parents went into hiding once the race began, worried that someone might use them to get to you."

"What do you mean?" Eva said, curious in spite of herself.

"I mean, if Stella got hold of your parents, they could be powerful bargaining chips."

"So you're saying . . ." Eva's heart skipped a beat—she had loved her aunt, spending a lot of her school vacations with her, helping out in her garden for extra pocket money.

"I'm saying that we're on the same side, Eva," Julia said. She stepped forward to give Eva a tentative hug. Eva didn't pull away but her face remained creased with doubt.

"Then why are we being held hostage here?" Lora asked.

"You're not," Mac replied. He looked around the room, there was now just the four of them. "Solaris reached out to me, so I went along with it."

"But," Lora looked puzzled, "what about the attack on the Dreamer Council in Paris?"

"An elaborate ruse," Mac said. "Everyone is fine. Well, OK, maybe a few of them got a little roughed up, but certainly no one was seriously injured. I needed to prove my loyalty to Solaris. And it worked."

Lora looked like her whole world had crumbled around her. "Does the Professor know?" she asked.

"No. No one knows but those of us in this room right now. I managed to release most of the Councillors but a few really are being held captive, which is an unfortunate necessity if I am to keep up my charade with Solaris. I have to make him think he has an alliance with me if I am to discover his plans."

"So, you're saying that you're on *our* side? This is just all a pretense? The Councillors in Paris, buddying up to Solaris, kidnapping us?" Lora sounded unconvinced.

"Yes," Mac nodded. "And it will all be worth it if it means we can defeat Solaris."

But in the meantime, can we trust you, Mac?

13

SAM

Sam landed heavily on the cobblestones of the street, rolling through the crash landing and into the wall of a row house. He tried to stand up quickly, but doubled back over and leaned against the wall, breathing heavily in pain. He felt his extremities, wriggling his fingers and toes, stretching his neck.

At least I didn't break a leg.

Sam could hear a strange hissing sound, and in the daze of his rough landing it took a moment to realize it was coming from him.

What the . . ?

Then he realized his Stealth Suit was rapidly deflating. It had inflated to break his fall and absorbed the impact, similar to an air bag in a car.

And I didn't even have to think about it. Nice!

He got to his feet and looked down the street at the exact moment that the large guy who'd been chasing him turned his way. Their eyes locked and in that split second they both recognized what it was they had to do.

Sam turned and ran, sprinting as hard as he could.

All I do . . . is run from . . . bad guys. Should make this an Olympic sport . . . I'd win a medal.

Despite his tiredness, Sam dug deep to run as fast as he ever had. The sun was now rising in the sky behind him as the hotel emerged in the distance ahead.

He risked a quick glance back. The guy was still there, not far behind. He wasn't gaining, but he didn't even look out of breath.

Gimme a break . . . how come the big guy's not puffing?

Sam tripped and tumbled into a messy fall, grazing his hands on the cobbled road and ending up breathless on his back. He sprang back onto his feet, determined not to give up—but he was spent. He stumbled and collapsed as he fell over a group of trash cans.

Sam got up once more and scrambled along the street, willing himself to run, but barely managing to walk. He heard the patter of footsteps getting louder behind him. He turned to look back, seeing the silhouettes of three figures set against the rays of the blazing sun.

This is it. They've got me . . .

But as they neared, Sam realized that these weren't the men who'd been chasing him.

These are Guardians!

They were coming to his aid with a very serious-looking Tobias close behind them.

"I'm sorry about, well, sneaking out like that," Sam said to Tobias. They sat in their hotel suite, the Guardians side by side at the door.

"You had me worried, Sam," Tobias said, clearly disappointed. "If you need to get out, if you're getting cabin fever or feeling stifled, that's fine, but let us know so that we can provide adequate security. OK?"

Sam nodded. "Where'd these guys come from?" he said, gesturing to the Guardians.

"Miami," Tobias said. "Well, they're based there. When we checked into the hotel I put out an urgent call to see who was close by. They showed up just after you left, I'm guessing."

"But who were those guys chasing me? They didn't look like Agents but they had Enterprise weapons."

"Local muscle," Tobias said. "Now in a local police cell."

"Is Stella expanding her empire?" Sam asked with a frown.

"Looks like she hired them and arranged to have them outfitted with Enterprise weapons and gadgets like these," Tobias said, inspecting a pair of the blue-tinted glasses that had enabled them to see Sam in his Stealth Suit. "She must have hired hands looking out for you everywhere now. Your ID is probably flagged at customs entry points throughout the world and when we came into the country, someone passed the word along."

"The joys of being up against an evil mastermind . . ."

"This is no joke, Sam," Tobias said. "She *is* evil. And you could have made things harder for everyone if they caught you."

Sam nodded. He was sitting at the open window, looking down at the street below, now busy with people going about their morning business.

"I've got something else to tell you," Tobias said after a long pause. "I received a call, from the Professor."

"Oh?"

"It's about Lora and Eva . . . they've been taken hostage."

14

ALEX

It is so cool that I'm allowed to go," Alex said to his mother as they sat on a flight to Vancouver. Six Agents sat all around them.

Phoebe didn't look happy to be accompanying Alex on a mission. In fact, she was flicking through a report, doing her best not to think about what danger might lie ahead.

"I mean," Alex said, "it's awesome that the Professor and the director—and you—trust me with this."

"Awesome," Phoebe said.

"Yeah . . ." Alex smiled as he looked around the cabin. People sat all around him in their seats, quietly filling in the flight time, oblivious to his mission.

If only they knew I'm heading off to help save the world. They'd all be thanking me.

"What are you thinking?" Phoebe asked.

"What? Nothing."

"Nothing?" she asked. "Then why are you smiling like a goose?"

"Geese don't smile," Alex said.

"It's a figure of speech," Phoebe replied. "Well, a figure of *my* speech, anyway."

"Well . . ." Alex looked around and then said, "these people have no idea who I am, or who you are, or what we're doing."

"That's the way it should be," Phoebe said, before adding, "we have no idea who they are, or what they're doing either."

"Yeah, but *we're* on a mission to save lives," Alex countered, a bit annoyed that his mother didn't share his enthusiasm for their important assignment.

"Alex," Phoebe said, "they could be saving lives too. They could be doctors, nurses, firefighters, soldiers, teachers—"

"Teachers?" Alex snorted. "Please."

"You don't think so?" Phoebe said, her voice taking on an edge. "They impart knowledge, the most powerful of all things. And you don't think that saves lives? It creates lives, it frees and expands the mind so that we can all have the chance to live out our destiny. The one you seem so eager to embrace."

Alex was quiet for a while then said, "Geez, Mom, I was just saying, you know, that I'm actually on a mission at last. I'm going to do something that will help us all."

Phoebe relented and smiled. "I hope so," she said, "but remember, Alex, it's not a game and it's not all about what you *do*. It's as much about *how* you do it, how you carry yourself."

"Is that your way of saying 'don't get a big head' about the mission?"

"That," Phoebe said, chuckling, "and just do what you can. This race is a marathon, not a sprint—we have a long way to go. You must be careful. If you really are one of the last 13, you will need to be ready, and safe. OK?"

"OK, Mom," Alex said and tried to smile like a goose again. "OK, got it."

15

SAM

"What does Mac want?"

"He wants you, Sam," Tobias replied. "Like everyone else out there, he wants you."

"And that's it? In exchange for Lora and Eva?"

Tobias nodded. "Two lives for one."

"Let's do it," Sam said, without hesitation. "Let's go now."

"You know I can't let you do that," Tobias said, smiling. "Though I admire your courage."

"But I want to," Sam said, standing by the door, ready to leave the room right there and then, to get to the airport and fly to Mac.

"Sam, we've got everyone we can spare on the search to find them, and believe me, we *will* find them and bring them home safe."

"And what, in the meantime we just carry on as if they aren't prisoners somewhere?" Sam paced. "We look for Maria, or we head back to the Academy, to find parts of this machine while our friends are in trouble?"

"We have a job to do," Tobias said, walking over to Sam. "And right now, it's the most important job in the world.

Lora and Eva are strong, you know that. And you know that they'd want you to continue doing what you are destined to do."

"Find the next Dreamer to get the next Gear," Sam said.

Tobias nodded.

"What if we did trade, though, and you tracked me? I mean, if I *don't* lead them to the next Dreamer, won't that mean that they won't find her?" Sam said urgently. "And then we could go and join the mission to find Lora and Eva, then come back here to find Maria?"

Tobias shook his head.

"Sam, they won't be so easily tricked. Our enemies are in some ways capable of more than we are—or, rather, would do things we would never consider doing. We believe they can see into your dreams," Tobias said. "You know that, don't you? Things have moved so fast that they are deploying every bit of dream tech ever invented, some of it highly dangerous to all Dreamers. It's how they're always close to us, aware of where we are and what we're planning. This morning has just proved again that they won't stop until they have you. They want to make you do what it is that you're destined to do—but for them."

"Yeah, well," Sam said, "I think I'm destined to one day practice my jujitsu against all those guys."

Despite the good-humored remark, Sam knew that Tobias was right. His dreams *were* becoming more and more unpredictable and dangerous. His enemies were emerging in them, trying to take control.

"We have to beat them, Sam. Lora would be furious if we wasted an opportunity to find the next Dreamer. Eva too."

Xavier and Rapha came into the room, yawning and stretching.

"You guys look like you've been up for hours," Xavier mumbled. "Hope you haven't been having too much fun without us."

"Not too much," Sam smiled. "But it's time to get ready and go find our next Dreamer."

"Soon enough, Sam," Tobias said. "We'll have to wait a few hours for some more Guardians from London to arrive—"

"We don't need more Guardians," Sam said. "Maria's right here, and if anyone else can see into my dreams, then they will know that too, and they'll be searching for her right now. We can't afford to wait any longer."

"You know that Maria's here? In this city?" Tobias asked.

Sam nodded.

"You're sure?" Rapha joined in, suddenly fully awake.

"Yes. I had the dream again last night and I recognized a statue from when we drove in from the airport. She has a boat out at the marina not far from here."

"That's amazing, my friend," Rapha exclaimed. "It is destiny!"

"Who knew bad weather would help us find Maria?" Xavier chuckled. "I'm loving us catching some breaks for a change. Nice work, Sam." He gave him a double thumbs-up.

"That *is* very lucky," Tobias said, but Sam couldn't help noticing how uneasy that revelation made him look. "OK. But if we do this with a small team, we do it fast—in and out." The two Guardians were seated by the door, waiting.

"I'm ready," Sam said, standing and putting his backpack over his shoulders and tightening the straps. "Let's go."

16

EVA

E va embraced her aunt warmly and felt tears prickle at the back of her eyes.

At last, something that feels like home.

After talking through it all, the reasons behind Julia being there, Mac's decision to pretend to side with Solaris, it started to make sense.

"If it is all true, that's pretty clever," Lora said. "By working with Solaris, you'll get the inside track on what he's doing and planning. We might finally get one step ahead and ultimately stop him."

"I appreciate you listening long enough to hear me out and to understand my plan. Thank you," Mac replied. "But I'm afraid that as long as you are on this ship, outside of this private room, it will have to appear that you are both prisoners here. I cannot be sure there are no traitors among my crew and staff who might divulge our secret before we are ready to act."

"I understand," Lora replied. "What will you do, with Solaris?"

"I'm not sure," Mac replied, sitting back into a plush

sofa. "I am intrigued by him."

"What does he want from you?" Lora asked.

"An alliance," Mac replied. "He knows I have connections, particularly in the military, and that we have a lot of technology around the world from when the US military was researching the Dreamer Gene. So I suspect he wants my resources."

"In exchange for?" Julia said.

"Solaris has offered his services as the frontline operator," Mac said, "to be out there chasing down Sam and the others, getting his hands on as many pieces to this machine as he can."

"But then what?" Lora said. "At what point will you stop him? You can't leave it too late."

Mac shook his head but said nothing.

But surely Solaris might expect that Mac would double-cross him, just as he knows that Mac would suspect Solaris of doing the same.

"How do you communicate with him?" Lora asked. "He's proven to be very elusive up to now."

Mac shook his head. "*He* finds *me*. There is no communication. He just shows up, usually when I least expect it. Intriguing, don't you think?"

"Intriguing?" Lora said. "You mean about his true identity?"

"That, yes, and more," Mac said. "Think of what we know in the prophecy of the Dreamers, know of Solaris I mean."

Eva said, "That he will rise . . ."

"At the time of the race," Mac added. "That's correct. But where did he come from? How was it that he showed up as the last 13 did? How can this ancient prophecy have known about Solaris? How could he be referred to thousands of years ago and then appear right on time? *That* is but one of the great mysteries of this race. Mysteries I intend to discover the answers to."

"How do you propose to do that?" Lora asked.

"By being patient," Mac replied. "The opportunity will present itself."

Eva and Lora shared a smile at the phrase they had used to discuss their escape.

"So," Lora asked. "What do *we* do?"

"We?" Mac said.

"What do you expect of us?"

"Ah," Mac replied, smiling. "Not now, but soon, I expect you to 'escape.'"

17

SAM

Sam told the street vendor to keep the change as he bought a bottle of water, then walked across the marina. The concrete jetties were full of fishing trawlers and charter boats, bobbing peacefully in the turquoise-colored water.

Behind him, Rapha, Xavier, Tobias and two beefy Guardians disguised as Cuban soldiers stood sentry, making sure there'd be no uninvited guests tagging along.

"I checked with the director back home, and he assures me they have no Enterprise-made Dreamers in Cuba," Tobias told Sam. "So it looks like Maria was naturally destined to be one of the last 13."

"Like me, right?" Rapha added.

"That's right—and Gabriella too," Tobias said. "You just have to convince her like you did them. And take it slowly so you don't scare her."

"Will do," Sam said, nodding. He adjusted his sunglasses and hoped he was wearing his best friendly face. He had changed his Stealth Suit to a Hawaiian shirt that Jedi would be proud of, along with some board shorts. His friends were dressed equally casually, while Tobias wore a white panama hat with an open-necked cotton shirt and linen shorts.

If this race to save the world doesn't work out, maybe we can go into fashion design with these Stealth Suits.

Maria's boat was easy to find. It was painted red, but it had faded and was weathering badly, the paint blistering and peeling away from the wood. Its name, the *Scaramanga*, was written in looping yellow writing along the large, flat stern. It looked exactly as it had in his dream. Maria did too—she was short, with a gentle face, her shoulder-length brown hair pulled back in a ponytail. She had the well-tanned skin of a local who lived out on the water.

Sam neared where she stood on the dock. She was facing his way, arguing fiercely with a tall, skinny man wearing dark clothes. Sam could only see the back of him, and out of nowhere an image of Solaris flashed into Sam's mind. He dropped his water bottle and ran towards Maria.

"Hey! *Hey!*"

The guy turned around—he was certainly not Solaris. He was wearing dark overalls, perhaps navy blue once but covered in black now, as though he'd recently emerged from a coal mine. He was an old guy with a craggy face and ratty beard.

"Hey," Sam said again as he joined them, trying to make it sound more like a greeting this time. The man and Maria both stared at him.

Sam said nothing. He felt awkward.

The pair looked to each other again, ignoring him and resuming their heated debate in Spanish.

Sam couldn't help himself and started to laugh. "Sorry," he apologized. There was something about what Maria had said, even though he couldn't understand it, which was universally funny—she was quite clearly giving this guy an earful. Maria stared back at Sam with fire in her eyes. The man was annoyed.

He turned back to Maria, pointed a finger at her and then at his watch, rattled a set of keys and walked off in a huff.

"What did he want?" Sam asked, but when he turned around, he saw that Maria was not standing on the dock anymore.

Huh?

Sam spun around but could not see her anywhere.

"Maria?" he called.

There was still no sign, so he called her name again, louder this time.

Maria emerged from below the deck of the *Scaramanga*, eyeing him suspiciously.

"Who are you?" Maria asked, more puzzled than anything.

"Sam," he said, smiling. "My name's Sam."

"And?"

"I'm, ah, well, I'm a friend."

Maria looked up and down the little dock, empty but for a crew refueling a small fishing trawler.

"A friend of who?"

"Well . . ." Sam found that he could not hold Maria's accusatory gaze—it was now both angry and questioning. "It's kind of hard to—"

"If you're after money, Sam, you'll have to step in line," Maria said sharply, turning her back on Sam and going to the little pilot-house on the deck.

"I'm not after money," Sam said, taking a foot off the dock and placing it on her boat.

Maria turned to face him, a spear gun in her hand, pointed at his chest.

"This boat is the last thing I have," Maria said. "So, like I said, if my father or his business partner owes you money, then you'll have to wait to speak to them about it."

"I—" Sam held both hands up. He couldn't look away from the spear pointed at him. "I just want to talk."

Maria lowered the weapon, but still held it ready. "How did you know my name?" she asked.

"That's . . . that's a long story," Sam said as he tried his best "don't-shoot-me" smile. "But I assure you, it's got nothing to do with money or anything about your father or his business partner. This is about you and me, and a load of important stuff. You know, like saving the world . . ." he said, lowering his arms and trailing off.

Maria nearly smiled. "Sorry, Sam, but I do not have a lot

of time. It is like I am, well, like I am living in a nightmare right now."

You have no idea . . .

"You see," Sam said, "that's just the thing."

18

ALEX

"There's been no sign of Stella," the Enterprise Agent said. "But she could be in there already."

Alex sat hunkered down behind a bush, next to his mother and the Agents, at a location about twelve miles north of Vancouver. He looked down at the complex below through binoculars. There were two tall fences, topped with razor wire. The second had signs saying it was electrified.

Alex scanned the scene from left to right. The only visible structures were a couple of box-like concrete buildings with broken windows dotted along their walls. The bare gray concrete was cracked. The adjoining desolate road and parking lot sprouted weeds through the asphalt and a tall water tower stood to one side. Eight large combat tanks were parked along one fence, with vines twisting all over them. They had obviously not moved for a long time. The abandoned military complex looked like a dumping ground, a graveyard for old, obsolete equipment.

"This place couldn't look more deserted," Alex whispered.

"Been that way for years," the lead Agent said. He

was a short athletic guy, wearing the same black combat fatigues as the other Agents assembled. They carried an assortment of weaponry strapped to their uniforms—dart guns, Tasers, stun grenades and handguns.

I guess they have to be prepared to fight fire with fire. I hope it doesn't come to that.

"It's still listed as a restricted military installation," the Agent continued, "a part of the NATO missile defense shield, but it's been mothballed all this time. Completely off limits."

"No sign of any recent activity?" Phoebe asked.

"None," the Agent replied. "What's your order?"

"We sit tight for a while," Phoebe said. "When we're sure it's clear, we go see what's in there. If Stella approaches, we apprehend her out here, *then* we go in to see what she's after inside. Either way, we need to check the site in case there's a Gear hidden there. It can't end up in the wrong hands."

"I should sneak in there now," Alex said. "Look around."

"*After* we know for sure that Stella's not there already," his mother countered. "Just wait a while."

"Look at all the Agents we have," Alex said, counting twenty in all. "They're capable of dealing with whatever Stella throws at them."

Phoebe looked to the lead Agent.

"Alex is right," he said. "We've got good cover positions out here, and we can send a team with him, a full protective detail. We have full schematics of the underground complex. We can execute this incursion with a high degree of safety and there won't be anyone else getting in or out as long as we control the high ground."

Phoebe looked to Alex, his eagerness obvious.

"OK," she said, finally relenting. "Set up security out here, put a lookout up on the water tower and we'll join your team. We go in now."

19

SAM

Maria looked at Sam, wary. They sat in silence in the cabin of her boat.

"How do you know all this?" Maria asked eventually. "Only my father and I call that tiger shark Scarface."

"Because I've been there before," Sam said, wondering why she looked so sad at this news, "with you, in my dream. You told me about it."

She shook her head. "No. You must have seen my father."

"I know it's hard to believe," Sam said. "I'm sorry, but that's the truth. And I've not seen your father."

"But how could you know of Scarface?" she insisted.

Sam hesitated, weighing up how else he could convince her. Out the window, at the far end of the dock where it met the beach, he could see his friends waiting.

"Where is your father?" Sam asked.

"I don't know," Maria said. "My father went missing out there, at sea."

"When?"

"Two weeks ago."

Sam swallowed hard.

Two weeks . . . did one of our enemies get here that much ahead of us?

"I'm still searching for him, every day," Maria said. "Well, until yesterday, when my boat broke down. Even my mechanic won't do any more work since my father owes money to everyone."

"Why?"

"He . . . he stopped fishing. Stopped taking on charters. He became obsessed with searching."

"Searching? What for?"

"He would never tell me," Maria said. "He just went out every day, diving and swimming and searching for something on the seabed."

"How'd it start? Did something happen that made him start searching? Some event?"

"Event?"

"A trigger," Sam said. "Something must have made him stop working and spend all his time and money looking for something under the sea."

"I . . ." Maria said, then she just trailed off and stared absently at the boat's weathered deck.

Sam didn't know what to say to her.

How can I convince her that she now has to join me in an urgent quest to find a Gear to an ancient machine?

". . . it was nothing really . . . but he did change after I told him about a dream I had. He was immediately convinced there was something there," Maria went on. "Some kind of treasure . . . he spent everything on it, buying new dive gear and equipment, and the last few weeks he sold everything we owned and borrowed money from everyone so that he could put all of his time and effort into searching for it."

Sam's jaw dropped as Maria's words sunk in.

"Maria," he said, slowly and deliberately. "In your dream—or nightmare—*was* there something you were looking for?"

She nodded.

Sam swallowed hard.

"Did you see it?" Sam asked. "In your dream—did you see what it was that you had to get?"

"It was shiny, made from metal. But . . ."

"When?"

"The night before my father started acting crazy. And then last night. I dreamed it again. It was a little wheel."

"Can—can you describe it?" Sam said, pacing anxiously. "Or, wait, can you draw it?"

He took a notepad and pen from his backpack and passed it to Maria. He watched as she sketched what was undeniably a Gear.

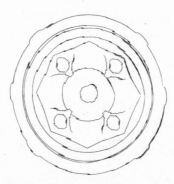

"That's it!" Sam said. "That's your Gear!"

"Gear?"

"A cog, part of a machine—part of *the* machine I was telling you about."

"Oh. *Oh!*"

"That's why I'm here, Maria, to help you get it. This is the 'treasure' your father is seeking. Everyone is. Only you could dream of it. We have to find it, and we can look for clues to find your father too."

And if Maria's father knew . . . others might. We may even be too late now.

"But how did he know?" Maria asked, confused.

"Your father must have known how important your dreams were," Sam said, skirting the issue. He didn't think now was the time to tell Maria that her father was probably a Dreamer who knew about the prophecy and had heard that the race had begun.

We'll cross that bridge later if we have to . . .

Sam stood and leaned out of the cabin door, signaling to the others to come down to the marina.

"Wait, Sam," Maria said. "If you mean for us to go after him, I'm afraid this boat, the engines . . . they are not working."

Sam changed his Stealth Suit to resemble exactly the oil and grime stained overalls of the mechanic before, and Maria gasped at his altered appearance.

"I have friends here who can help out with that," Sam

said. He went up on deck with her and waved along the jetty at the others. "I think you'll find with their help, this boat's going to run like she never has before."

20

EVA'S NIGHTMARE

I'm walking down a city street. It's a weekend, I'm sure, and I'm going shopping. I'm alone, but due to meet my family—my aunt. I look for her at the food court in the mall. She's not here yet. I sit and wait. I check my phone. A missed call from Aunt Julia.

I call her back.

A voice answers.

Metallic. Menacing.

Solaris.

"If you want to see your aunt again," the voice says, "come outside."

The line goes dead. I walk through the masses of people, frantic, scared. I'm aware of my surroundings and things aren't what they seem—the people, the stores—none of it's real.

"I'm in a dream," I say. "Just a dream." I try to slow my breathing.

Be in control.

Outside, it's not the parking lot that I'd walked through just before.

It's a barren endless desert. I turn to head back but there's nothing but sand dunes behind me.

No—there's a figure, in the distance, distorted by a heat haze. I run to the person.

I clamber up the last sand dune and see the figure, now laid prone on the baking ground.

Looking around, this is still the only sign of life as far as I can see. I watch the figure on the sand. The person is lying still and has been for a long time judging by the sand coating them. I approach slowly as I get closer. I bend down and turn the person over. They are wearing the face mask of Solaris, but the outfit doesn't match—it's a Stealth Suit. I pull the mask off.

Professor?

EVA

Eva stayed in the shower until she felt free of the memories of her nightmare. Once dressed, she sat on the edge of her bed, waiting. The room on the freighter was small, but like the rest of the ship it was recently refurbished and comfortable.

Tap, tap, tap.

Eva opened the round porthole and poked her head out.

Lora's head was sticking out her window.

"Talk about déjà vu!" she laughed. "You OK?" she asked when she saw Eva's face.

"Yeah," Eva said. "Just had a bad sleep. Nightmares."

"Anything you think will be happening soon?" Lora said, concerned.

"No, it was a pretty out-there dream about—"

There was the sound of the key at Eva's door.

"Someone's here!" she called, then pulled back into her room and sat down on the edge of her bed, playing the role of captive as a guard entered.

"Follow me," he barked.

Eva followed the guy out into the hall. They stopped outside Lora's room and he unlocked her door, giving her the same order.

"So," Lora said, as they trudged along between a couple of guards, "I guess we're finally going to be doing something."

"This here," Mac said, pointing to a large backlit blueprint on a table in his private office, "is the facility in Vancouver where we pioneered the genetics research. The US army like to do their secret research on foreign soil."

They were alone in the room, just Eva and Lora along with Mac and Julia, which meant that they could talk freely.

"The site has been closed for years," Julia said, "but it's still of use in this race."

"Why?" Lora said. "How? I mean, what's there that

could possibly help us now?"

"A supercomputer was at the complex when the lab was shut down. It was considered obsolete and left behind," Mac said.

"OK, so what does it do?" Eva asked.

"It's not what it does, it's what it *holds*," he replied. "Which is everything to do with our Dreamer gene research."

"And they just left it there?" Lora said. "I find that *very* hard to believe."

"It was considered a shut-down program," Mac replied, "and keeping all this under lock and key at the site was an initial measure of security that was eventually forgotten about. And I believe there is information stored within it that might help us find the last 13 Dreamers ahead of time, and perhaps even better navigate their dreams to find the Dream Gate first."

Eva and Lora exchanged wary looks.

"I know how this sounds," Julia said, "but I worked alongside Mac there when I was just starting out as a biochemist. The Enterprise gave me the chance to advance, nurturing my career and taking me on as an Agent once the facility closed down."

I never knew her at all, until now.

"So I know a little about what went on there and I honestly think Mac might be onto something. He told me of his plan to trick Solaris and to retrieve the missing data so I decided to help him."

"You really think that this information could help us win the race?" Eva asked.

Julia nodded. Mac was silent, reading their faces for a reaction.

Eva turned to Lora. "Then we should go and at least see what's there. Lora?"

Lora looked resolved. "OK, let's do it."

21

SAM

The *Scaramanga* powered through the bright turquoise waters of the reefs and islands off the southern coast of Cuba.

"This is amazing!" Maria said, steering the boat through the water. "It's never gone this fast!"

Sam gave her a thumbs-up. On the rear deck, the two Guardians were wiping off grease and oil, having managed to remove the old diesel engine and replace it with a V8 turbo engine from a speedboat they'd bought with cash, all in less than two hours. The result was the wooden-hulled *Scaramanga* cutting through the water at a speed it had never been designed to cope with.

Hope it holds together.

"Scans reveal that there's no radio activity where we are headed," Tobias said to Sam. A laptop and satellite dish were set up on the forward deck, where Xavier and Rapha were readying the dive gear.

"Good," Sam said to Tobias. "And in my dream you weren't all here. It was just Maria and me. So things have changed."

"As Solaris figured in your dream last night," Tobias agreed, "it's good to change things up—what's the benefit of seeing the future if you can't alter things to be more in your favor, right? We must prepare ourselves."

Tobias nodded towards Maria, who was still piloting the boat, constantly checking their location on a GPS navigation screen.

"You need to talk to her about her dreams some more," Tobias said. He held up his phone and pointed it at her, showing Sam the screen. It was just like the glass walkway at the Academy's Swiss campus, showing the outline of the body glowing with a spectrum of colors. Maria's aura was a sparkling yellow with flashes of silver.

"I'll take over piloting the boat," Tobias said. "Talk to her, see if she can tell you anything more about where we need to go."

In the living quarters below deck, they sat in a room that had bunk beds on one side and a little table, booth seats and galley kitchen on the other. Maria poured ice water from a cooler.

"I need to know about your dream," Sam said. "About when you saw the Gear."

Maria shook her head fiercely. "I don't like talking about my dreams. I told you already, I will show you where this wheel is that I saw. I think I know now. That is enough."

"But this dream, was it a *nightmare?*"

Maria paused and tears formed in her eyes. She sat down on the seat opposite Sam, but just stared at him and said nothing for a long time. Finally, she sighed.

"Yesterday, when the boat broke down," she said, "it took the whole night to find there was a problem with the fuel lines, about eight hours. Then I slept for maybe an hour. I thought it was the fumes from the engine room, but it was a nightmare like I'd never had. So clear, so real, but . . . how do you say in English . . . *not* real? Impossible but somehow true . . ."

"Surreal?" Sam offered.

"Yes. Surreal."

Maria sipped her water, and Sam could tell from that familiar distant look he'd seen on so many Dreamers' faces that she had gone back there, into the Dreamscape, reliving what had happened.

"I dreamed I was diving, at the place I had last been with my father, but this time with someone else. A boy. I don't know who—he was wearing the diving gear and I couldn't see his face clearly. But the current at the edge of the reef where the seabed drops away took me—it whipped me along and I could not stop, I was flashing by with the fish and turtles, and after a while I just went with it, relaxed." She paused and looked at Sam.

"Go on," he encouraged.

"So I thought, in my dream, that I might just float along with the current and somehow end up at the Barrier Reef or somewhere crazy like that—it felt like a fantasy. But after a while I realized that my air supply was running low, so I used my spear gun to shoot at a coral reef as I passed, then pulled myself in on that cord. I held on to the reef, reloaded the spear and then repeated the process, over and over, until I hauled myself to the other side and out of the fast-moving current. And there . . . there is where I found the wreck."

"A shipwreck?"

"Yes, a shipwreck," she said. "It is what my father went out to search for, when I had a nightmare about it before. I have seen this ship in my dreams many times lately, and again last night. I could see this wheel—your Gear."

"What's the wreck?"

"A Spanish ship. One of maybe twenty vessels lost to a hurricane from the 1502 Columbus expedition."

"And you saw that in your dream?"

Maria nodded.

"Did you enter the wreck?"

"Yes . . . I think so," Maria said. "My dream went by in little flashes, like a broken memory, or like watching a movie and skipping every few minutes. The last thing I remember was being inside an underwater cave, then I was inside an old wooden ship. There was a room, I heard noises, like running—there were people there but I couldn't see them. I felt afraid though, like people were after me. I kept running through the ship in the dark, and I came into a room of treasure. I held that wheel, that Gear, in my hand, before . . ."

Sam frowned, waiting for her to continue. "Before . . ?"

Maria just shook her head.

"What happened in your nightmare, Maria?"

"I was not alone in that room," she whispered.

Sam let that detail be for now as he asked, "And you dreamed where this location is? I mean, you can remember it?"

She nodded hesitantly.

"Could you find it again?"

"I think so. I could follow the edge of the reef and find the wreck." Maria looked at him. "We have to go there, don't we? You really think that this is a true thing, my dream?"

"Yes," Sam said. "So do you believe me now?"

Maria looked out the porthole to the sea. "I have hope, so yes, I will believe, for now. For my father," she said. "He was, *is*, a brilliant diver. He can swim like a fish. He knows these waters, and every danger—including the sharks, and Scarface."

"What are you saying?"

"I think that he is alive," she said.

"But . . ." Sam pointed at her father's underwater hand-held propeller drive, recovered from one of Maria's earlier searches. Its yellow paint had been indented with the unmistakable pattern of teeth marks.

"I know," Maria said. "But in my dream, he's still alive. He helps me."

"How?"

"I . . . I am getting chased, by a figure in the shadows."

Sam thought of Solaris.

"And," Maria said, "to get away I have to travel through a small, tight space. I'm scared of it—of what chases me, but also of this small way out. I feel such fear."

She's claustrophobic—frightened of being in small spaces.

"My father tried to help me out," Maria said. "That's when I woke up."

"*Tried* to help you?"

"There was not enough time . . . he was screaming too."

Sam nodded, understanding. "And the Gear?"

"I didn't have it," Maria said. "He did. The figure in the shadows."

ALEX

Getting past the security fences and the alarmed, password-coded doors was an easy process. With the Agents' insider knowledge of the complex, they practically walked straight in. Alex watched in awe as one of the tech Agents used a small laptop computer to crack the PIN code in a matter of seconds.

I so gotta learn how to do that!

It was getting into the underground complex undetected, in case Stella and her crew were already inside, that was the hard part.

"OK, this isn't creepy at all," Alex said, walking with a flashlight to light the way under his feet. The downward-sloping corridor was long, dark and damp. Water sloshed under their feet, and was soon around their ankles. He looked back at the entrance door, which was ajar, and the sunlight peered through. Four Agents walked in front of Alex and Phoebe, with Rick, their commander, leading the way. He looked strong and capable, a determined look in his dark eyes. Alex eyed the fierce tattoo on his left arm as he strode into the complex. A couple of Agents cautiously followed behind. More Agents remained outside, keeping watch. Phoebe kept close to Alex.

"The tunnel takes a few turns up ahead, then we start heading further down," Phoebe said, consulting the schematic on her handheld screen.

"Further down?" Rick said. "But the water is getting deeper and deeper already."

"It'll be OK," Phoebe said, "once we clear the sealed doors to the complex proper."

The troops up front stopped at each corner, carefully scouting their way ahead in case there were any surprises lurking in the doorways or adjacent corridors.

"This is it," Phoebe whispered, her voice echoing in the space.

"It's a . . ." Alex's voice trailed off as he leaned forward to look down into a cavernous hole that disappeared into the pitch-black far below. The groundwater beneath their feet trickled over the edge like a gentle waterfall. "What *is* it?"

"Elevator shaft," Rick said. He took a couple of glow sticks from a zip pocket, cracked them to life and dropped them down the shaft.

Alex watched as they fell, taking several long seconds to hit the bottom with a sharp thud that echoed loudly back up the shaft. Alex winced at the clattering noise it made in the eerie complex.

"Well, it's not flooded," Rick said. "Must have landed on

top of the elevator, which is down there, probably the full fifteen stories."

Phoebe pointed to a cobweb-covered control panel on the wall. "Can you bring the elevator up?"

Rick motioned to the tech Agent. He pulled out an electric screwdriver and had the elevator's control panel off in seconds.

"It's unlikely," the tech Agent said. "This is hooked into the emergency grid, so I can route the backup generators to here, but there's no telling if they'll kick over if they haven't been maintained."

"Where are they?" Phoebe asked.

The Agent shone his flashlight over the schematic diagram, flicking at the screen to see more details.

"Back that way and a few access levels down," he said.

"Take two Agents with you—try those generators," Phoebe said, looking at the schematic once again. The tech Agent and two others ran off the way they'd come.

Phoebe turned to Alex. "Do you feel any different?"

"What? No," Alex replied, shining his flashlight around the elevator shaft. There were metal ladders set into two opposite walls running down the shaft as far as Alex could see. "I feel completely normal."

"Nothing looks familiar? No déjà vu?" Phoebe prompted.

Alex shook his head. It was so quiet, only the sound of the falling water could be heard as they waited for the Agents to hook up the power. Alex looked around, trying harder to concentrate on his surroundings. He touched the open, slide-across metal gates that had once blocked the opening for this massive elevator. The closing latch was cut through, the two sections bright and sharp.

Someone's beaten us here.

Alex said, "Ah, guys . . . *look*." He pointed to the severed lock on the elevator gates, the shiny silver metal glinting through the rust and dirt, even more noticeable under the illumination of the flashlights. "Looks as if someone recently cut through the lock," he said.

"I don't like it," Phoebe replied. "We should move."

"Go back?" Rick asked.

"No. Down. There's another way out," Phoebe replied, shining her flashlight over the ladders in the elevator shaft, then checking the complex's schematics. "I have a feeling this is going to get real interesting, real fast."

SAM

"**M**aria is convinced that her father is still alive," Sam said to Tobias as the two of them suited up to dive. Maria was explaining to Rapha and Xavier how to operate the boat.

"Maybe he is," Tobias said, checking his air regulator. "I think it's likely Maria's father is a Dreamer—and a powerful one at that—who understood what her dream could mean. He may be just lost. And he may not be coming back, so we need to keep an eye on Maria in case she falls apart out there. I know she is concerned about his disappearance, but to find the Gear we don't need her father—we need Maria. You need to remain focused on why we are here, Sam, and help Maria stay focused too."

Sam nodded.

"We're ready," Maria said, walking over to them.

"OK," Sam said to her. "I guess there's no time to feed the sharks today?"

Maria looked at him, puzzled. "No, not today, I think."

Sam smiled.

"Are you ready?" Maria asked, before pulling on her mask.

"Yep," Sam said, donning his air tanks.

Maria gave the diving OK sign and pointed to the water. Sam and Tobias pulled on their face masks and respirators and they all gently toppled backward into the warm sea.

They followed the reef to where it met the shelf in the seabed before dropping away into deep black water. Sam tried not to imagine what might be hidden in the darkness. They had tanks with enough air supply for two hours' dive time and they each held personal propulsion units. For now, the small torpedo-like machines were unnecessary, the trio rocketing along with the current, but the units would be invaluable for breaking out from the powerful water flow.

Sam followed Maria's lead, Tobias behind him. The reef teemed with sea life, the colors of the fish and corals almost too bright and varied to take in. After five minutes of being swept through the water, among schools of reef fish and small sharks darting curiously near them, Sam saw Maria changing direction. He continued to follow her closely, pointing the propulsion unit to his left and squeezing its trigger so that the propeller whirred at full bore and carried him out of the current. Tobias followed suit. They passed over the reef and to the other side, where the water was clear and calm.

Maria slowed to a stop and the three of them came together. She pointed to the bottom of the reef where it met the sand of the seabed. Sam gazed down and as he stared, more and more details emerged. The coral there had grown in thick, uneven patches which Sam realized sprawled over the wreck of a ship.

But Sam knew from Maria's description that it was not the wreck that they were after. This was a big ship, metal, clearly made in the last century. Not the five-hundred-year-old wooden wreck that they were searching for. The vessel was on its side and Maria pointed to a large open cargo hatch.

Really? In there?

Sam followed her, the propulsion unit leading the way. The hatch was crusted over with marine life and crabs scurried to escape as they entered. Inside the cargo bay, he pressed a switch on his handgrip that turned on a light. The space before them was huge.

Maria was getting further ahead, moving through the water like a fish, but Sam was wary about snagging himself on the wreck. He checked over his shoulder and saw that Tobias was about a body length behind.

The ship's cargo area was vast, every surface covered in barnacles. Sunlight shone through the open loading hatches above, highlighting seaweed that hung like curtains from the rusted deck. Sam pushed through, spotting Maria's flippers ahead. They reached the end of the cargo bay and went through a doorway and long corridor, heading down the ship's internal staircase.

Sam spluttered water and a shower of bubbles as a huge

eel flashed right in front of his face mask. Tobias bumped into him as he pulled up in fright.

Tobias gave him a thumbs-up, his eyes knitted in concern. Sam nodded and they carried on, catching up with Maria by zeroing in on her propulsion unit's light.

She's clearly used to swimming with far better divers.

They passed through the engine room, the massive mechanical axles populated by crabs and crustaceans that scurried away from the brightness of their lights.

Maria stopped at the end of the room. In the rusty back wall was a hole that seemed to go on forever—an endless void not much wider than Sam's shoulders. At first Sam didn't understand what he was supposed to be looking for, then it dawned on him.

This must be the entrance to the underwater cave she told me about.

Even through the mask on her face, Sam could see Maria's panic. Her breathing quickened dramatically, bubbles flowing fast around her and her body tensed up. Sam reached out to touch her shoulder lightly. He pointed to himself and then to the hole, indicating that he could go first.

Maybe that'll help with her claustrophobia.

She shook her head determinedly and ducked down to swim into the inky underwater tunnel.

OK, then.

The darkness ate up their lights and soon, maybe

twenty yards in, the tunnel narrowed to the point where it was only just wide enough to navigate forward. Sam could feel the sharp barnacles and shells that covered the surface catch against his skin.

Well, there's no turning back in here.

Sam felt his air tank scrape along the top of the tunnel and his vision was reduced as he powered on through a cascade of bubbles from Maria's respirator in front. Finally, the tunnel widened out into a bigger tunnel, nearly big enough to drive a small car through.

An underwater car, that'd be cool . . . or a submarine.

Sam forced himself to concentrate on what was ahead. It was too easy to tune out, to get lost in the strange beauty of the surroundings. He slowed his unit as the tunnel curved ever so slightly, then seemed to start to incline.

The dive was long and made it difficult for Sam to keep track of time. What was probably five minutes of pushing through the tight confines of the tunnel, felt like an hour.

It's like I'm floating through a dream . . .

Abruptly the tunnel opened up further into a large cave. The sudden change in light reflecting around the huge space startled Sam and the propulsion unit slipped from his hands. It stopped automatically and drifted idly forward in the water. He reached forward and caught it, gripping it tightly again and kept on after Maria, now just a small speck of light up ahead.

As he swam, he could make out the cave floor

below—the walls barren but for tiny shrimp that lived in the murkiness, their glowing bodies making them look like some kind of alien species from another planet.

Up ahead, the light got brighter, making Sam's eyes squint after becoming accustomed to the pitch darkness. Sam slowed and Tobias appeared beside him. Here the large cave split into two. Maria seemed to hesitate and then took the large opening to the right. It was big enough for the three of them to swim side by side and the tunnel inclined further upward.

More light shimmered through the water ahead.

Is it the surface of the sea? Can't be. We're still too far down. It must be the top of the cave.

Their three rays of light bounced back from something in the darkness beyond. Sam felt a sense of dread mingled with surprise wash over him as he broke through the dark surface of the water and felt a blast of air hit his face.

ALEX

"Almost there," Alex quietly called up to his mom.

Phoebe followed him down the ladder. It was painfully slow going. "There's a reason I was never that keen on being in the field," she muttered.

"Four more rungs and you're there," Alex said, standing on top of the freight elevator, the glow sticks at his feet. Rick was inside the elevator with four Agents, having gone down through the hatch. Two Agents remained at the top of the shaft providing cover should anyone be following their path through the complex. "That's it."

Phoebe let out a sigh as she stood on the top of the elevator alongside her son.

"I guess it's a family trait that we don't like heights, eh?" Alex said.

"Yep."

"Well," Alex said, "if it makes you feel any better, I wasn't as scared knowing that you were doing all the worrying for both of us."

"Anytime."

Alex laughed.

Rick popped his head up through the access hatch in the elevator roof. "Let's get moving."

Alex helped his mother down through the hatch and quickly followed her.

"See," Alex said. "That wasn't so—"

A loud whirring noise interrupted Alex and then the world went white.

Inside the elevator, the control panel lit up, as did the fluorescent lights on the ceiling. Alex could see a corridor through the open elevator doors, and lights blinked on one by one, dominoes of brightness in the subterranean maze.

"Power's up," Rick said, taking out a serious-looking automatic dart rifle. He spoke softly into his mic and held a hand over the ear that contained a tiny earpiece. The lights in the elevator went out again.

"OK, we've got the generators up, but there's only enough fuel to run the power for maybe an hour," Rick said, "half that if we have to use the elevator to make it back to the surface, so let's do this quick."

The Agents nodded and started off down the corridor, the lead pair scanning with their stun weapons. Another Agent held the complex's schematics on a tablet screen and directed the team with hand signals. Soon they were taking twists and turns through tunnel branches. Alex made sure he stayed close to his mother.

Funny, Mom worries too much about me, and I'm just as worried about her.

"Most of what's down here is not related to the Dreamer program," Phoebe explained quietly as they jogged along a corridor.

"Old military stuff?" Alex said.

"Something like that," Phoebe replied.

"This is it," one of the lead Agents said, stopping at a vault-like door labeled *MAJESTIC 12*. The door was made of polished steel and had an old-fashioned numerical keypad on one side.

"Do you have the swipe card?" Rick asked Phoebe. "Or at least the code?"

"We have *a* code," Phoebe said, entering numbers from information on the schematic and pressing "Enter." The keypad flashed red and let out a loud repeating beep. The door stayed locked. "OK, I expected that. Have the team upstairs try to route around it."

Alex inspected the keypad as Rick spoke into his tactical headset. The keypad looked standard enough—the screen above it indicated that a four-digit code was needed to unlock the door. It reminded Alex of the kind of codes he and his friends had hacked dozens of times on each other's phones. Changing the wallpaper to an embarrassing boy-band picture and installing matching ringtones had been a juvenile, but fun, hobby.

"There's no response from up top," Rick said, changing channels on his radio headset and calling for the team.

"What does that mean?" Phoebe asked, looking concerned.

Rick said, "Could be just the concrete between us interfering with our tactical mics . . ."

"That's unlikely with our tech. Could it be something else?" Phoebe said.

Rick nodded, looking worried. Alex saw the other Agents tense, and they didn't need to be told to head back down the tunnel and set up a defensive perimeter against unwanted guests.

"If you've got a screwdriver, I can open this door," Alex said, taking his phone from his backpack and holding out his hand. Rick passed over a screwdriver.

"Give me two minutes." Alex undid the panel and searched for the wire he thought he'd jack into, but it wasn't in there.

This keypad system looks . . .

"It's older than you are," Phoebe said, as if reading his mind.

"I'll figure it out," Alex replied, sorting through which wires went where, then finding those that fed into the computer board controlling the locking mechanism. "OK, this should do."

He stripped the wires and fashioned them so they could be connected to the end of his headphone jack, then plugged it into his phone. He tapped away on his hacking app, working as fast as he could, eager to get out of this dark, eerie dead end.

"We've got company!" an Agent down the corridor called to them, making Alex jump. "They're hostile!"

Then the shooting started.

Phoebe bumped in close to Alex, drawing her dart gun defensively.

The numbers on Alex's phone whirred.

"Eight, three . . ." Alex read off the screen frantically.

"We're outnumbered!" an Agent yelled, moving backward and shooting with his dart gun on full-auto.

"Two . . ." Alex murmured hurriedly. "Come on, come on!"

"Argh!" an Agent fell back, slumping against the wall. A stun grenade rolled from his hand and Rick kicked it down the corridor.

KLAP-BOOM!

"Got it!" Alex shouted.

CLICK!

The door in front of Alex made a series of churning noises and swung open. They dived inside.

SAM

Sam broke the surface of the water and swam over to sit on a rocky outcrop, catching his breath after taking off his air regulator and face mask. Shafts of light pierced the gloom, casting a strange green glow around the cave. The low ceiling was covered in stalactites with steep walls circling all around and a vast tranquil pool in the middle.

He knew they were still underwater—they had emerged into a giant underwater cave in the middle of the sea. Sam pointed his light across the pool to illuminate the other side of the cave. Part of the wall looked to have collapsed in on itself.

"Dios mió!" Maria said.

"It's incredible!" Tobias added.

Sam turned around and saw in the midst of the gloom what looked like an ancient pirate ship, marooned on a steep bank of sand.

I don't believe it . . . a ship on a beach under the sea?

Sam pulled off his dive gear and stood next to Maria on the rocks opposite the vessel.

"It really could be an old Spanish galleon," Maria said in

awe. She shone a flashlight along its keel, sunken into the sand. "It looks good as new."

"*This* is what you dreamed?" Sam asked.

Maria nodded, her mouth agape.

"Look here," Tobias said, pointing his flashlight at the sand between the small rock pools that ran along the edge of the cave on the other side.

Sam and Maria hurried over the rocks to join him.

"Footprints?" Sam said, looking at them.

Maria crouched down and studied the markings in the sand.

"My father!" she said. "He must have made it here!"

Sam felt instantly on edge and looked around. There was no sign of anyone else.

Footprints don't mean it's her dad. Who else might have been here?

"Papá!" Maria called. The sound was gobbled up by the empty space of the huge cave. "*PAPÁ!*"

There was a rumbling overhead, and dust and debris filtered down from the ceiling near the caved-in section of the far wall.

"Um, maybe don't do that again," Tobias said quietly and Maria nodded.

"Where'd you go in your dream?" Sam asked her.

"Up there," she said, pointing her light up onto the ship at an ancient-looking cargo net made of ropes. "I climbed the shrouds."

"Shrouds?" Sam asked.

Maria said, "That's what they're called. They hold the masts steady. But see here, they've broken away, so now they're hanging over the hull. Good for climbing up, right?"

Sam looked around. The ceiling was only a few yards from the top of the boat's deck and there was certainly no room in here for masts.

Where are they?

"It looks like the boat was stowed away in here, perhaps to weather a storm and it became stuck in here by a cave-in," Maria said, shining her flashlight all around. "Let's get on board."

"OK, I'll give it a try," Sam said. He clipped his flashlight to his belt and reached out to the first rung of rope. The ancient ship felt cold to the touch, the ropes wet and slippery. Sam hoisted himself up onto the first rung which held firm under his weight.

"Maybe this won't be so—"

Sam's foot fell through a rotten rope rung in the ancient shroud net.

"—bad."

"Watch your footing, Sam," Maria said, close behind him.

"Yeah, thanks, nice tip," Sam replied. "You should take extra care, Tobias."

"What are you saying?" Tobias said with a chuckle.

"Nothing, you just have the greatest mass of the three

of us," Sam said, and he heard his old science teacher laughing.

Sam climbed higher until he was level with the first row of cannons. There was another row of hatches above that and then the deck. He flicked on his flashlight and shone the beam through an open hatch. Inside he could see a long room with a low ceiling. Sam sized up the hatch. He could get through, but it would be a tight squeeze and the wood floor inside might be rotten.

"Keep climbing!" Tobias called. "Get to the deck."

Sam looked down and nodded. Tobias stood there with his flashlight illuminating the way for Sam to keep climbing up the shroud net. Maria was shining hers around the rocky sand, looking for more footprints.

"Here I am," Sam muttered, "climbing aboard a five-hundred-year-old pirate ship in an underwater cave. Another day in the adventures of Sam—"

His hand pulled through a rotten rope and he slipped down before catching himself.

"—the Great."

He reached the balustrade at the side of the deck and hauled himself up to it. It seemed sound and he swung his legs around so that he was sitting up then flicked on his flashlight.

"Ah, guys . . ." Sam said.

"What do you see?" Tobias called.

"Looks old," Sam called back. "Dry and dusty. Lots of

bats were here, I think—now long gone. Maybe there was a small opening somewhere in the cave."

"Be careful with your footing," Maria called up. "The deck may be fragile."

"Stick to the edges!" Tobias said. "They'll be the strongest part."

"Got it!" Sam replied, and he dropped his legs down, his feet crunching through the dry, dusty remains of a long-abandoned but well-used bat toilet. "Here I am, on another adventure, ankle deep in centuries-old bat poo . . ."

"What'd you say?" Tobias called.

"I said," Sam called down, shuffling along with his feet, "that it seems OK. You guys can come up. I think this is what they call the poop deck."

Sam went to the side and shone the flashlight down the rope ladder. Maria put her foot on the first rung, getting ready to climb. He took a step to the side to get a better angle with his light.

CRASH!

Sam fell through the deck.

Sam coughed and kept his eyes shut against the dust, feeling around for his flashlight. He felt the base of a cannon, which he traced blindly with his hands, feeling the way to the open cannon hatch. He stuck his head out, breathing in the clearer air outside the ship.

"Sam!" Tobias said urgently but quietly for fear of triggering a cave-in. "Are you all right?"

Sam nodded his head, still settling his heart rate and breathing. The white-gray dust cascaded from his hair and face with the movement. He continued to suck deeply at the fresh air outside the ship.

"I fell through the deck . . ." Sam said.

"Yes, we heard," Maria said, halfway up the rope net. "I'll come up to your level, climb through a cannon hatch."

"Go slowly," Sam replied. "The air's thick inside here, dust everywhere. Can't hardly see, let alone breathe."

Tobias stayed down below, rummaging through his dive pack and pulling out some stick flares. He broke one and set it upright into the sand, the cave illuminated in its bright-red glow.

"I'll come up in a minute," he said, and he once again held his flashlight to help Maria with her climb up the net. Maria fitted easily through the first cannon hatch, but she quickly reappeared, leaning out and coughing against the dust storm still inside. She shone her flashlight down over the net for Tobias to make his ascent. Sam watched as the rope net gave out under Tobias' weight three times, but he eventually made it all the way up to the deck level above.

"I'll scout around up here," Tobias called down.

"Stick to the edges," Sam yelled out, "where the boards will have more support."

"Ha, ha," Tobias said with a mock laugh. "You two work from the bottom deck up. The Gear could be anywhere but keep a look out for navigational equipment."

"On it," Sam said, looking down the ship's length to see Maria still peering out of a hatch like he was. "Maria, can you remember where to search for the Gear from your dream?"

"Not exactly—it looked like a stateroom, but that could be anywhere."

"OK. Well, you check that way and I'll go down here," Sam suggested, pointing to the back of the ship.

"Sure," Maria replied, disappearing for a moment, and then emerging again. "The dust has nearly settled."

"And tell me if you see anything that might be recent," Maria said to them. "Any sign of my papá."

"Got it," Sam said.

Sam shone his flashlight around the ship. He could not see Maria up ahead inside the lower gun level through the haze, but could easily make out the beam of light from her flashlight sweeping around. Sam inched towards the stern. There were large cannonballs in neat rows in wooden holders, wooden crates and lots of tools, and a wooden wall with a door that creaked open.

They put this in a cave to weather out a storm, and what— just left it here? It makes no sense. I mean, where would the crew go without a boat?

By the light of the flashlight, Sam could see that he was in a storeroom. There were empty barrels and caskets, sacks of dried beans petrified with age, and jars and bowls scattered all over the floor.

The far wall had another door, which led to a room with two smaller cannons, pointing out of the back of the boat. He pushed open a hatch and could see outside to the little rocky outcrop from where they'd come. The flare continued to burn and light up the cave. Beyond the tranquil pool of water, the caved-in part of the wall loomed up into the darkness. The more Sam stared from this closer vantage point, the more detail he could make out. Wood beams stretched from one side of the rocky stone wall to the other, tethered together with ropes. Smaller boulders, stones and mortar filled the gaps making up the wall.

That part of the wall looks like it's man-made.

"Guess that accounts for the missing masts," Maria

said, standing next to Sam.

"Why would they do that?" Sam said.

"Run their ship aground in here and then make sure it's hidden away?" Maria said.

Sam nodded. "And spend all that time and effort to block up the entrance. Even with a full crew, that would take days, weeks maybe."

"It's a mystery," Maria said, shrugging. She went to a ladder leading up to the deck above. "Come on."

Sam followed her up the ladder to the next gun deck, which was equipped with more small cannons. At the far end of the deck were the crew quarters. Everything in there seemed stripped bare.

"Looks like the crew took everything they could," Maria said. "Maybe they hid the ship here so as not to lose it to an enemy, or sink it, and they planned to come back and get it later."

"But how did they get away? On another ship?"

"Maybe. Many of the early explorers and crew would get sick or die, so they probably had more ships than crew for the return voyage. And for some reason, they never came back."

They walked along the gun deck to the stern, navigating through a jungle of ropes hanging from the ceiling, and then took the stairs to the upper decks. From the main deck, Maria peered down through the Sam-sized hole that ended two decks down.

"Maybe you've been eating too much chocolate," Maria said to him with a smile.

"Hey!" Sam replied. They headed for the rear cabin, where the door was open and the glow of Tobias' flashlight was dancing around inside. "So you're saying I'm heavy?"

"You are the only one who has fallen through the deck."

"Yeah, well, that was a weak point in the wood or somethi—"

Sam's foot shot through another rotted-out wooden deck. He delicately pulled it back through the splintered wood, trying not to make it worse for himself. Maria laughed as they entered the small, dark room.

"This looks like the first mate's cabin," Tobias said without looking their way. He was studying the contents of a large cabinet. "The captain's cabin is probably beyond that door."

Sam looked to where Tobias shone his light. "So you haven't been through there?" he asked.

"It's locked," Tobias said. "I'm looking around for a key or something we can use to—"

There was an almighty crash and Tobias and Sam snapped their heads around in unison, in time to see Maria kick the door off its hinges.

They both looked at her, speechless.

Maria smiled sweetly. "We want to get in, don't we?"

27

ALEX

The heavy doors clunked shut behind them and Alex locked them manually, his hands still shaking and his breathing unsteady.

"That should hold them for a while," Alex said.

"Can't they hack the code like you just did?" Phoebe asked.

"Not without this," Alex said, holding out a small silicon chip and putting it into his pocket.

Rick swiftly tied up the arm of a wounded Agent. Another was on the ground, dragged in by his comrades but out cold. The others were nearly out of ammo.

The lights flickered noisily overhead, off, then on . . . then off again, for good.

Darkness. They turned their flashlights back on.

"Could it be Solaris out there?" Rick asked.

"Could be, but Stella seems to be doing his dirty work so it's more likely to be her," Phoebe said.

"I'd sure like to have a word with her, if it is," Rick said, gritting his teeth in anger. "But we'd need more ammo to take her down."

"There were too many of them," Phoebe said.

"What is this place?" Alex asked, taking several paces down the corridor and looking through a glass wall into . . .

Is that a lab?

He walked further down until he found a door and entered. "It looks like a science lab. Or maybe some kind of medical lab."

"Gene research," Phoebe said, coming in to stand next to him. "In its time, it was the most advanced genetics lab in the world."

Alex didn't reply. He felt sick. Before him, along a wall, were tall glass jars full of . . .

What are they?

"During the gene research here in the 1950s and 60s," Phoebe said, "they were experimenting—"

"On *people*?" Alex interrupted.

"On creating Dreamers," Phoebe corrected.

"Then these are all . . ." Alex's voice trailed off as his flashlight hovered over the glass containers.

"Early prototypes," Phoebe said with a sad voice. "Those who didn't make it."

Alex was lost for words.

"We gotta hustle!" Rick called into the room. "They're cutting through the door!"

"Come on," Phoebe said, putting an arm around her son. "Let's go. We need to search the offices and see what's there."

Alex let himself be led away from the macabre sight before him, though he couldn't help but feel guilty. He had survived to become a Dreamer with a loving mother, when so many before him had not lived to see or experience anything of life at all.

As they hurried back down the corridor, Alex turned to see sparks erupting through the cut in the door.

"Hurry!" Rick yelled. "Faster!"

Room after room, lab after lab, Alex and his mother searched, seeing more things that Alex didn't want to know about. Phoebe led the way through the laboratories, repeatedly asking Alex if he felt any sense of having been there in a dream.

"If there is a Gear here, I don't think I'm going to find it," Alex said. "We should focus on getting to the vault and finding the code book. Seeing all this is making me feel sick."

"Sweetheart . . ."

"No!" Alex said. "All this was part of some Enterprise program to create Dreamers like me. And I'm here today because of it, right?"

"It's more complicated than that."

"Is it? Or is it really simple?" Alex said. "I see it as some-one was here playing God. Playing around with DNA. Experimenting in the dark. It's . . . it's disgusting. How could you sign up for this?"

"All this gave me you, and for that I am grateful," she said.

Alex looked away. "Come on," he said, "let's get out of here."

Back out in the corridor, Alex saw that Rick and his men had built a barricade of steel cabinets and tables in front of the door.

"There's nothing here. We have to find another way out!" Phoebe called to Rick.

"Two minutes!" an Agent called out. Alex looked over and saw the sparking burn of the blowtorches. They were nearly through the door.

"We're out of options," Phoebe said to Rick.

"Agreed," Rick said.

"OK, come with me, Alex," Phoebe said, examining the schematics of the complex. "We have to follow the emergency air shaft out. There's a coded door near the top of the ridge where we should be able to get out."

"We can't leave them here!" Alex said.

Rick smiled and put a hand on Alex's shoulder. "Yes, you can."

"You're outnumbered—"

"We're trained for this," Rick said. "We'll hold them here as long as we can, then blow this exit and follow you out. *Go!*"

28

SAM

The captain's stateroom was impressive. Compared to the small, cramped dark rooms of the rest of the ship, this was spacious. It stretched the full width of the boat and had shuttered windows all around. There was a bed in one corner, a hammock and bench seat. Cabinets lined the walls filled with journals, keepsakes, supplies and clothes, and a large desk stood by the rear windows.

And one captain.

"That's . . ." Sam said, looking at the skeleton in the chair behind the desk.

"Amazing!" Maria said.

"Disgusting," Sam said. "Eurgh."

The two of them peered at the dust-covered skeleton from a distance, all the color sucked out of his clothes from five centuries of salty air.

"How'd he die, do you think?" Sam said.

"Too much booze," Tobias said, picking up a bottle from the table. "This stuff will kill you."

"Oh," Sam said. "Maybe he decided to stay with the ship to protect the Gear?"

Maria's expression changed and she cocked her head to one side before walking towards the desk and the skeleton. She began opening the desk drawers, checking through each one carefully before moving on to the next. Sam and Tobias stood still, watching her.

"Maria?" Sam said.

She said nothing, continuing her meticulous search, going through the many drawers one by one, running down the sides of the desk. When she got to the last one she shook her head in frustration and began the search again, starting at the first drawer.

"Maria?" Sam said again.

She stopped, as though glued to the spot next to the captain. "I know it's here. It feels familiar, but different. I think—I think I can't remember my dream so well."

"That's OK," Sam said. "Take your time."

"Remember, it may not look exactly like you saw it," Tobias added. "It may be a part of something else."

Sam moved around to the back of the desk and began searching cupboards and drawers behind. He was careful not to get in Maria's way or distract her as she tried to recall the details of her dream more clearly.

"Ah, guys . . ." Sam said.

Tobias looked over to Sam, then Maria.

Sam said, "Take a look at this."

Sam kept his light on the top of the desk, where a piece of paper rested in the dust. It certainly was not from the sixteenth century. It was written in Spanish in marker pen, and the only word Sam could understand was the first—*Maria*.

"It's from my papá!" Maria said excitedly.

"What does it say?" Sam asked, looking at the Spanish words, uncomprehending.

While Maria read the note, Tobias held his smartphone over the letter, using an app to translate.

> Maria,
>
> If you have found this, it means that you are searching, for me or that which you have dreamed of. I tried to spare you the danger but I have failed. I cannot stay any longer to search. I have some supplies to make a raft. I will follow the islands home. Be careful.
>
> Love, Papá.

"I knew it. He's alive!" she shouted, and the noise echoed inside the room.

"I don't understand. How'd he get into this room?" Sam said, looking back at the door that hadn't been opened in five hundred years until Maria had smashed it down.

"Through here," Tobias said, and Maria and Sam joined him at a window where a little grapple hook with knotted rope dangled down to the sand.

"So what do we do now?" Sam asked.

"We call our friends and we carry on looking for the Gear," Tobias said. "Tell them to wait for us while we start island hopping in search of Maria's dad—sorry, what's his name?"

"Chris," Maria said from across the room.

"We search for Chris."

"Use my phone," Sam said, taking his large handset from his dive bag.

"Ah, that's an oldie," Tobias said, looking at the huge phone Sam held out to him. "We used them in the field way back when. Jedi give you this?"

Sam nodded. "Actually, better not. Jedi made this one bite a little."

"Ah, I can just imagine," Tobias said, pulling out his own phone and dialing.

"Guys?" Maria said, from behind them.

Tobias' face changed as he listened intently on the phone, then a moment later he looked at it, then ended the call.

"Guys?" Maria repeated.

"What's up?" Sam said to Tobias, guessing it was something serious.

"Everyone on Maria's boat has been placed under guard

by some Cuban coast guards," Tobias replied. "It seems they're acting under someone's instructions."

"Sam!" Maria said. "Look."

"Stella?" Sam asked, too alarmed to answer Maria. "Or Hans?"

"Xavier didn't say. He had to get off the line before they noticed. He did manage to tell me that one of the Guardians made a distress call to the Academy. So backup should arrive from the US and hopefully the Professor can pull some diplomatic strings too," Tobias replied. "But they sure can't help us right now. We're as good as marooned down here."

"Guys!"

Sam and Tobias finally looked at Maria. Light glinted from the object she was holding in her hands.

The Gear!

"This is it," Maria said. "It's more beautiful than I dreamed."

Sam reached over and traced over the numeral with his finger. They shared a knowing smile.

Eight. We're really getting there.

"Now we go and find my papá," Maria said.

"But how did you . . ." Sam said.

"I just felt that I had to look inside the captain's jacket, and it was there."

"Genius," Sam said.

"We need to get out of here," Tobias said.

"How?" Sam asked.

"I don't know . . ." Tobias replied, looking lost. "I don't know."

"I do," said Maria. "We have to follow my father's footsteps."

EVA

"**H**ere we are," Mac said, pointing down to a sprawling complex on the edge of an industrial park.

Eva looked out the window as the helicopter came in to land. The place was overrun with rust and weeds and other signs that it had long ago been abandoned. A row of rusted tanks stood like statues inside the perimeter of the security fence. Their pilot touched down on the asphalt of the desolate parking lot. Mac, Julia, Lora and Eva climbed out of the aircraft, heads low, and ran to the nearest building, where eight men from Mac's security detachment waited.

"We got here late," Mac's security chief said. "We found a few men out cold."

He passed a dart over to Mac, its sharp end snapped off.

"Looks like Stella's here," Mac said. "And she's up against the Academy and the Enterprise. We must move fast."

"We've found another way into the complex," the chief said. "The air ducts, up near the ridgeline."

"Then let's go," Mac said.

The security team formed a protective circle around the four of them as they moved towards a dense tree line.

"Great," Eva said to Lora as they followed Mac and his men towards the trees. "Now we're going in there against our own. Can't you warn them?"

"Communications are down," Lora said, having gotten her phone back from Julia. "Just stay close to me."

"OK, I guess we just have to get this done quickly," Eva replied.

Mac chuckled. Eva looked at him, puzzled and agitated.

"Just like your mother," Mac said by way of explanation.

"You *know* her?" Eva asked.

"Yes, a wonderful woman," he said. "One of my best researchers."

"She worked for you *too?*"

"Oh yes," he replied, "alongside Julia. In her capacity as an Enterprise Agent, she was charged with raising you. But in her own right she is one of the greatest analytical minds I've ever come across. And her own dreaming genes were a perfect fit for our DNA manipulation."

"Sounds like I was a lab rat," Eva said.

"No, my dear," Mac said. "Like I said yesterday, you are enhanced, nothing more. I just gave you a little extra oomph with your dreams is all. The rest is your parents and what they passed on to you and taught you."

"This is it," the security leader said, and they stopped at a concrete box the size of a dumpster with steel vents built into it.

"We're going into *that?*" Eva asked.

"It would seem so," Mac said. "I need to see the supercomputer and data banks for myself and you may prove helpful down there."

"Me?"

Mac looked to Lora. Sparks began to fly and the earsplitting noise of grinding rang out as the security team cut away at the vents with power tools.

"Really," he shouted to Lora over the din, "what *do* you teach them there at the Academy?"

"What's he talking about?" Eva said.

"The Gears," Lora said, and Mac nodded. "When near one, it is possible, just *possible*, that it may prompt a sense of déjà vu in the last 13. Mac, this theory isn't—"

"Really?" Eva said. "But I haven't felt anything with the gears at the Academy. I'm not one of the last 13 . . ."

"It's more likely to be a subconscious connection, Eva," Lora explained sympathetically. She leaned in to whisper, "We noticed a change in your dream patterns which might be related to being close to the Gears."

Then she turned to Mac. "So you think there is a Gear here, inside this complex?"

"I doubt it," Mac replied. "But there is a vault containing some relics from past Dreamers and it would prove useful to have Eva on hand in case we get lucky."

"OK, then," Eva said to them both. "In we go."

"I guess I'm not that surprised," Mac said, standing in the ransacked vault. "Someone else was bound to have the same idea."

"Who?" Eva asked.

"Possibly Stella," Mac replied. "Or maybe that swine, Hans."

"But the data you're looking for is right here, sir," the security chief said, pointing to an ordinary-looking gray box in the corner. "We can still retrieve it."

"Excellent! Pack it up, take everything you can get your hands on. I want to examine it all." Mac turned to Eva and Lora. "Though that does rather beg the question—what were the others looking for? What else was in this vault?"

"We don't have the time to consider that now," Julia said. "There may still be other interested parties down here. We should take the data and go."

Eva and Lora followed the team out, guards quickly stepping in behind them. Suddenly the lights came back on, blinding everyone in their flickering glare.

While it was good to be able to see, Eva couldn't help thinking, *how come I still feel so in the dark about this place?*

SAM

"We'll have to swim back the way we came and make for the next island. There's no other way," Tobias said.

"Maria?" Sam asked. "What do you think?"

"That could work," she said, sitting on the edge of the captain's desk, her father's note in her hands. "We have enough air in the tanks, I think."

"That way we could remain hidden underwater," Sam said. "We could get to the next island undetected. We can't go back to our boat. Chris' raft is the only way we can leave."

"Hmm," Tobias said. "If they haven't already, whoever has paid off the coast guards will likely have divers in the water soon, which means that they'll be hot on our tail. And even if they don't, they'll run us down in their boats, track us via our air bubbles . . ."

"What about the way my father got out of here?" Maria said, smiling.

They turned to look at her.

"I don't think he swam out," she said. "I think he climbed out onto the island beyond."

"Sounds good. But what we need," Tobias said, a plan forming in his mind, "is a distraction."

"Distraction?"

Tobias broke into a huge smile. "Yeah, a distraction!"

Tobias' idea of a distraction was nothing short of crazy.

So crazy that it might just work.

"Yep," Tobias said, setting alight a tiny test pile of gunpowder in a brass bowl. "This powder is still good."

"But the cannons . . ." Sam said. "They might not work."

Tobias loaded one of the small ones, propped it up towards the cave's ceiling, and lit the fuse.

BOOM!

The cannon belched the shot and blasted a small hole through the ceiling, creating a shaft of bright sunlight. The sound reverberated through the cave and pieces of rock rained down on the water around them.

"That answers that question, then," Sam grinned.

The three of them immediately set to work moving one of the small cannons facing the front of the cave, replacing it with one of the larger ones, its bigger barrel barely fitting through the hole.

"That wall they built to hide this ship," Tobias said, studying the walled-off area before them, "it's made up of the wood from the masts and is netted together with the rigging ropes. They must have then piled the ballast stones up to make the wall, and mixed up a sandy mortar to pack it all together. I'll blast through it with this cannon like a sneeze through a tissue."

"Lovely," Sam said. "But it does sound great in theory."

"You blast away at the wall, and you manage to shoot through it—then what?" Maria asked. "What about the Cuban gunboat guarding your friends—you'll go to war against them with sixteenth century cannons?"

Tobias looked around the room.

"I've got plenty of ammunition," he said. "And I'm in a fortified position. I reckon I can hold them out there for a while—long enough for you two to get out and swim to the next island," Tobias said. "Find Chris and get the Gear away from here on his raft. Or flag down a passing boat and contact the Academy. Lay low until backup arrives, OK?"

Sam and Maria nodded.

"Good luck," Tobias said.

"You too," Sam replied, then he and Maria went back to the captain's quarters. They slid out the window and shimmied down the knotted rope. They took their dive equipment to the bow of the ship, where the rocky walls of the cave started up a steep incline towards the small hole of daylight created by Tobias' test fire.

"We'll pull our dive gear through the hole with ropes," Maria said.

"Got it," Sam said.

He watched as she climbed the rocks, agile as a mountain goat, wriggled through a crevasse, then reappeared above, dropping down a rope. Sam tied on the first set of dive gear and Maria hauled it up. They repeated the process with the second. Finally, Sam tied off the two prop units, then ran to the rock wall to climb. He pushed through the small hole made by the cannon, squinting against the bright daylight outside the cave. As he came to stand next to Maria, Sam realized they were exposed in an open expanse of short grass.

"Let's go!" he said, pointing to a clump of trees and shrubs ahead, heaving the equipment across his shoulders.

As they ran for cover, the first cannon shot rang out behind them.

31

Sam swam next to Maria, gliding effortlessly through the water—a pair of human submarines powering through the water.

And no one knows we're here . . . thanks, Tobias.

Now about six feet down, Sam was completely settled, breathing through the regulator, his arms outstretched like Superman in flight as he let the propulsion unit do all the work, dragging him forward.

They passed over corals and saw modern wrecks, most likely small fishing vessels. Sam marveled again at the abundance of life in the water. It was like the New York City of underwater worlds—all manner of creatures, living in their own city, the corals their skyscrapers and the wrecks and sandbars their own distinctive neighborhoods.

The seabed eventually gave way to open sand, rippled by the powerful currents. It slowly began to angle upward. Sam followed Maria's lead as she switched off her propulsion unit and they let the gentle surf wash them ashore.

"We'll probably have to ditch our dive gear here, won't

we?" Sam asked, dragging off his tank and seeing that his air was almost gone.

Maria didn't answer. She already had her dive gear off and was searching along the sandy beach.

"Papá?" she called out. "Papá!"

No answer came from the tiny island. It was shaped like a boomerang with a total area no more than three tennis courts. She ran on, weaving through the sprinkling of palm trees, Sam following close behind.

"I don't think he's here," Sam said, catching up with her at the highest point. She was staring down at the base of a tree. Sam followed her gaze and saw the charcoal remains of a fire.

"No," Maria replied, crouched down. "But someone was."

"You think this fire was him?" Sam said.

"I hope so."

"Look!" Sam pointed at the base of the palm trunk.

MARIA —

LA PRÓXIMA ISLA

Sam looked to Maria. "What does it say?"

"My father has gone on to the next island. Let's go!" Maria said with a broad grin.

They ran back to the beach. In the distance Sam could see several boats just off the coast of the original island and heard the deep cough-bang sound of cannon shots echoing across the water.

Time to blow the wall and make a getaway while they wait for the dust to clear. Come on, Tobias, get out of there.

Keeping low, they darted across the island. Maria pointed to the next spot they were headed—a barely discernible speck against the horizon.

"We'll stay at the surface of the water," Sam said. "The waves will hide us."

"You can swim this?" Maria said, picking up her flippers.

"Still got a bit of power in this," Sam replied, hefting the propulsion unit.

"Follow me. And keep your eyes open and stay alert," Maria said, flushing out her face mask before putting it on.

"Tough reef around the island?" Sam said, adjusting his flippers.

"Yes," Maria replied. "But this is also Scarface's territory."

EVA

"We're not alone down here!" Julia said.

"Hurry," Lora said. "Whether it's Solaris or Stella, we don't want to be caught in a tight space like this with only one way out!"

They ran through the labs, Eva hesitating as she saw canisters and cabinets full of all manner of experiment specimens gone wrong, in all their stark reality, under the bright lights.

"Quick!" Julia said, pulling Eva along.

At the bottom of the air ventilation shaft, Eva and Lora were clipped into the harnesses they'd used to descend.

"Now's your chance to get out of here," Julia whispered into Eva's ear. "I'll keep them distracted, you and Lora run for it. Don't stop for anything."

Eva grasped her aunt's arm, words sticking in her throat.

"I know," Julia said. "Me too. Don't worry, I'll see you soon."

And before Eva could say a word, she was whisked away, the ropes pulling her straight up through the shaft towards the distant light above.

Eva ran through the woods, Lora close behind her. They didn't stop running until they came to two fences topped with sharp wire and a red sign warning that they were electrified.

"Over there!" Lora said, pointing off to one side where a tree had come down and had fallen across both fences.

Eva ran for it.

WHACK! WHACK!

Darts hit Lora's Stealth Suit but they were only glancing blows.

Two of Mac's security guys were hot on their heels. Another two lay unconscious near the top of the shaft, taken out by Lora's swift combat skills.

"Here!" Lora said, touching Eva's arm. In that instant, both their Stealth Suits disappeared. *They* disappeared.

"Optical camouflage," Lora said. "A Shiva add-on. *Go*, keep running!"

Eva ran over the fallen tree like the balance beam she used to train on as a gymnast in school. Once over the fence they ran down the hill, quickly coming to a road that wound through the woods.

"Listen!" Eva said.

A truck was coming, its engine loud and near. It appeared around the corner. It was a logging truck, straining with a full load, driving slowly down the hill.

"Come on, we're hitching a ride," Lora said. "Quietly!"

Eva readied next to Lora and as the truck came closer they saw that the two security guys were emerging from the woods and nearing the road.

"Start running!" Lora said. Eva followed her, sprinting behind, the optical camouflage lost as they ran.

Lora latched on to the truck's load tray and reached back. Eva grabbed on to her wrist and felt herself being lifted from the road. She reached out with her other hand and seized a chain wrapped around the logs.

Looking back, the guards stood in the middle of the road, watching in defeat as the truck picked up speed.

The two of them climbed up onto the logs, gasping for breath.

"We made it," Lora said.

"Where do we go now?" Eva asked.

"Wherever this truck stops next," Lora replied. "And we call home."

Eva ate her salad and Lora had a third refill of her coffee. The diner was busy, full of truckers mostly.

"So we wait here?" Eva asked.

"We're only a few hours from Vancouver," Lora said, "and a team of Guardians should be here before long."

Eva nodded.

"You did good back there," Lora said with a smile.

"You're the one who knocked out those other guards," Eva said.

"True."

"You'll have to teach me some of those killer moves."

"Anytime," Lora laughed.

SAM

Sam's prop unit died out after a couple of minutes motoring along on the surface of the water, headed for the next island. Maria's was still running and she powered onward, not knowing Sam was floating behind her, unassisted, in the middle of the sea.

In Scarface territory.

No propulsion, no air tank. No one else around. Great.

Sam looked down into the water. These two islands were much further apart than their first swim, and the water was deeper in this midsection of the stretch—so deep, he could not see the bottom here at all. Everything below just disappeared into a deep-blue haze.

Who knows what's lurking down there?

Despite himself, Sam began to panic. He let go of the prop unit, which floated away. His arms and legs thrashed in the water as he readjusted to his new weight without the prop unit.

"Calm down," Sam said to himself, spluttering out water and lying on his back to float, looking up at the sky. "Keep cool . . ."

When he felt still and calm again, he turned in the water and saw Maria, now just a little dot in the water ahead, still being pulled along towards the next island. Sam rolled over onto his back again and set off after her in a leisurely backstroke.

If Scarface wants to chomp on me, better I don't see it coming.

Settled into his rhythm, Sam turned and adjusted his direction every thirty strokes. Then something bumped into him—

"Argh!"

Sam spun frantically in the water.

"It's me!" Maria said, her hand on his arm.

Sam nodded, coughing out the water that he'd swallowed in a panic.

"Sorry," Maria said, treading water next to him. "I didn't notice you weren't with me. Your prop unit is dead?"

"Yeah, a while ago."

"Mine too. We're nearly there, though."

Sam looked around. The island was close, maybe sixty yards away. The closer they were to the sandy beach, the more surf they encountered. The swell of the waves lifted them high in the water.

"The reef comes up below us," Maria said. "And closer in, it's near the surface, see the breaks?"

Sam looked to where she was motioning and could see there was foaming white water as the waves hit the surface of the reef at low tide.

"That's sharper than you imagine," Maria said. "The coral will cut right through your wet suit—and you. Can you make it around the far side, if we go to the right?"

Sam looked at the view ahead and nodded, but Maria was lost as another large swell raised him up and down in the water.

"Yeah," he said. "Sooner we're on land, the better."

"Come in next to me," Maria said, and she swam slowly, watching behind, and Sam did the same. "Here it comes— ride it and steer to the right."

Sam didn't have time to reply, he had to move fast, swimming as quickly as he could to keep abreast of Maria as the wave rose up, taking them both bodysurfing.

Sam let out a whoop as the water powered him along. He kept his arms outstretched in front of him as the wave grew higher and gained more and more momentum, pushing them onward, towards the reef.

Maria was to Sam's right, and slightly ahead, the wave taking her across exactly as she had described. But he started to fall behind, and despite leaning hard to the right, the wave had other ideas.

"Maria!" he called out, just before the wave broke in two where it hit the underwater edge of the reef. Maria kept going the way she'd planned while Sam was spat towards the white foaming reef ahead. He decided to take evasive action and took in a huge lungful of air.

He dived *down*.

The reef was close, the water bubbling and churning. He rose to the surface and took a breath, checking the waves. The next few swells looked smaller. Sam thought he could roll with them across the worst of the reef—as long as he made it over before the next big swell hit.

Sam swam as fast as he could. His arms ached and twice he hit his flippers against the reef. He felt one flipper tug away, breaking free, and he could feel himself slow down from the loss of momentum.

The next crashing wave pushed him up and he was tossed over the edge of the reef.

Made it!

The other side of the reef was a tranquil lagoon of shallow water and Sam rode the fading waves onto the beach. He crawled ashore and lay on his back, exhausted. He didn't know how long he stayed like that, perhaps five minutes or more, until he heard his name being called.

"Over here!" he called back wearily, waving an arm up in the air. A moment later he heard footsteps squeaking in the sand and he took off his mask and looked up, seeing Maria standing over him, the sun behind her. "It's cool, I made it."

"Just."

"I know," Sam said, showing a defeated grin. "I'm done in. Can't swim another stroke. I am cooked."

"I mean," Maria said, pointing to his feet, "that you were

lucky you made it to shore in one piece."

Sam sat up and looked down at his outstretched legs.

His right flipper, which he thought he'd lost, was still on—but it was now no more than a shoe, the flipper past his toes entirely missing.

"What the . . ?"

"*That*," Maria said, "is how Scarface says hello. Next time you won't be so lucky."

Sam swallowed hard.

Maria offered her hand to help him up. "Come on," she said. "This island is much larger than the last, and we've got some ground to cover by nightfall."

"Papá!" Maria yelled. "Papá! Are you here?"

"Chris!" Sam called out. "Chris!"

Maria emerged from the thick foliage and stood before Sam. She looked defeated.

"Maybe we missed him," she said.

"Have we covered the whole island?"

"There's only the far west coast left," Maria looked beyond the shrubbery and pointed. "And then there's a long sand-bar leading south. It's the only break in the reef. It's close."

Sam looked up at the sky, now heavy with cloud and the oncoming night.

"Then let's hurry," he said. "We might need to make a shelter. Looks like there's a storm brewing."

Maria looked at the tall palms that shot up through the thick green growth, swaying in the gathering wind.

"You're right . . ." she said. "Come, the calmest coast is to the west anyway."

"And we can check the sandbar," Sam added.

"If my papá is still here, he'd have seen this weather a long way off and be sheltered there already."

They trudged through the big-leafed shrubbery which turned to prickly grasses and then low succulent ground cover that squelched and crunched underfoot.

"Eggshells," Maria said. "The seabirds breed here, watch where you step."

Sam did as he was told. The birds' nests were dug into the sand, some as deep as an arm length. The sand in most places was so encrusted with years' worth of birds making this their home that it was hard and brittle—until you stepped too close to a nest and it crumbled away.

"Argh!" Maria took a tumble.

Sam helped her to her feet, she dusted herself off and they walked on, following the setting sun.

"Least it's not hatching season," she said. "You wouldn't believe the smell of this place when it's full of birds."

"Yeah, think I'll give that a miss," Sam said.

A few minutes later they crested a small sand hill and the greenery resumed. Down below Sam could see that the palm trees ringed the waterline on a beach that twinkled with the setting sun on the water.

"We'll start up that end of the cove—" Maria said.

"Wait," Sam said, putting a hand out and catching Maria's pointed finger. "You smell that?"

She sniffed at the air, then nodded. "Smoke."

"A fire," Sam said. He couldn't pick out any smoke against the graying sky, but then a crackle of wood popped and hissed and sparks flew up into the air from the direction of the beach.

"Wait!" Sam said in a shouted whisper, running after Maria as they bounded down the rise. "What if it's not your—"

"Papá!" Maria called, running out into the clear expanse of the beach. "Papá!"

"Maria!"

Her father stood up from where he sat by a fire and ran to Maria. They embraced warmly. Sam stood by them as they hugged and cried, feeling a bit awkward. Their reunion made him wonder about his own parents.

Not parents—Agents. Where are they now? Do they miss me? If I saw them now, would our reunion be this warm?

"Papá, this is my friend Sam," Maria said, finally pulling away from her father to make the introductions.

Chris walked over and shook Sam's hand.

"Sam helped me find you," Maria said. "And he . . . it's a long story."

"Well," Chris said, looking up at the sky as thunder rang out. "I think tonight, my dear, we have nothing but time. And food."

He pointed to a stack of coconuts to drink, as well as a couple of large fish, gutted, cleaned and skewered on sticks ready to roast over the fire.

"I used a piece of net I found washed up," Chris said with a huge smile. His eyes looked tired from days of baking sun and sea salt. "I caught them this afternoon. I think our reunion tonight was meant to be."

"It's a feast," Sam said, sitting down by the fire.

How much does he know? I know he's a Dreamer, but can he be trusted?

Chris looked thin and gaunt, having spent nearly two weeks on his own between the islands, eating what he could scrounge from the sea and land. Sam watched as Maria and her father caught up, busying himself cooking their dinner as night fell.

"I made a shelter under those trees—it should hold against this storm," Chris said, pointing to where he'd improvised his raft into a roofed structure thatched with leaves. "It's safe here. We are in the most sheltered of the bays, and there's no way a boat can come ashore to this side of the island, day or night."

Sam nodded silently and turned the fish.

"So," Chris said, "tell me about you—Sam, was it?"

"Yeah . . ." Sam said, trying to work out in his mind where to begin and how much Chris might know.

Well, this guy's obviously worked out a lot himself and he should know all about me. Here goes.

"My name is Sam. I'm one of the last 13."

"I knew that Maria was special," Chris looked at Sam with wonder, "ever since she began dreaming of the wrecks out here. I knew it couldn't mean nothing. I was trying to help her, to make it safer. I didn't want them to come for her."

"So you *are* a Dreamer," Sam said to him, "and you know all about the prophecy?"

Chris nodded at Sam.

"Well," Sam said, "Maria's a part of it now."

Chris turned to his daughter smiling. "So what did you find?"

Maria took the Gear from her dive bag. "Here it is."

Chris took it gingerly from her and cradled the Gear in his hands. "It matches your drawing. Well done, querida mía."

Sam looked closer at the tiny Gear.

"Do you know what it's for?" Sam asked him.

"I've heard rumors," Chris said. "There's been talk of little else lately among Dreamers," he added in reply to Sam's questioning face. "It's part of a machine, isn't it?"

"Put together with the twelve other Gears," Sam explained, "they complete a machine—a kind of navigational device made by da Vinci."

"And the machine will reveal the hidden place where the greatest treasure lies—the Dream Gate. That's it, isn't it?" Chris said.

"Papá . . ." Maria looked at him. "You know of this?"

"Yes," he said. "I'm sorry I didn't tell you—I was trying to protect you."

Maria looked a little unsure, this was all moving so fast for her.

"How many of the Gears have you recovered so far?" Chris asked Sam.

"This is the sixth," Sam said, thinking back to the golden key he'd found at the start of the race inside the Star of Egypt and all the pieces since. "We don't have all of them, though."

"Solaris?"

Sam nodded. "He wants to create the machine himself. And there are others now—do you know of someone called Stella, from the Enterprise?"

Chris shook his head. "No, I don't think so."

"She's the Enterprise operations leader," Sam said, "or she was. She's gone rogue and is working with Solaris. She attacked the Academy campus in Switzerland and the Enterprise headquarters in Silicon Valley. After the attacks, the Academy and the Enterprise formed an alliance to go up against their enemies together."

Chris lifted his eyebrows in surprise, but his gaze stayed lost in the hot coals of the fire. "Very strange times indeed."

In Sam's dive bag was his dart gun, which he tucked into his belt as he changed back into his Stealth Suit. He had excused himself and drifted away from the fire, leaving Maria and Chris to talk through everything alone.

Sam finally got enough signal to use his phone to call the Academy, wishing he had called earlier. The switchboard put him through—

"Bonjour?"

"Zara!" he said to the French Dreamer. "Any word from Tobias?"

"No," she said, "is everything OK?"

"I'll explain later, I promise. Where's Jedi?" he asked.

"He's here. He finally got a trace on your phone so help is on the way."

Sam said, "That's good news. The sooner we get out of here, the better I'll feel."

"Did you find the Gear?" she asked.

"Yeah, and a whole lot more besides," Sam replied, looking over to Chris. Sam thought back to what had happened in the Sorbonne with Zara and her father, who had gallantly fought off Hans' men while Sam and Zara made their escape in pursuit of her Gear. "How are your parents doing?"

"They're OK. They're staying here in London. Papa is recovering after having his legs set, and my mother is reading a lifetime's worth of novels. Never seen them happier, actually."

"See, it all kind of works out," Sam said. "So how far out is our ride?"

Zara replied but a thunder clap broke above Sam and the sky immediately opened up with a torrential downpour.

"Zara, I missed that. Say again, how long?"

Sam couldn't hear her. He thought he made out "— hours," but couldn't hear anything more. She may have said two or ten for all he knew.

There was another rip-crackle in the sky and the connection was lost. Sam ran over to join the other two under the shelter.

"Should have put the fire under cover," Chris said as the last of the embers were extinguished.

The thunder boomed so loudly that Maria screamed and the three of them covered their ears and shrank further back into the shelter.

"I sure hope you built this thing to code," Sam yelled, as the woven fronds and grasses of their ceiling bucked and flapped against the storm. Chris and Maria hugged one another. As the storm raged overhead, Sam realized just how much he missed his own parents, and decided in that moment that when the storm cleared, he'd try to make contact with them.

After all, we're in this together now.

ALEX

"**Y**ou sure this is the way?" Phoebe called after Alex.

"Yes!" Alex said, pausing at the end of a corridor to check the schematic. Three doors ahead gave them three options. "We need to—"

The lights went out and they stayed out.

"Hang on," Phoebe said, zooming in on the schematic on her screen. "We're where?"

"Here," Alex said, tapping the diagram. "Ha! You know, this kind of reminds me of the Easter egg hunts you used to organize for me."

They laughed—

The sound of an explosion and gunfire came from down the corridor where they'd just been.

"This way," Alex said, pushing the door open on the right, to the larger of the rooms. "We're right at the vault now."

"Wait!" Phoebe said as soon as they'd entered.

Alex shone his flashlight to where Phoebe stood.

"Someone's been here," Alex said, pointing to the gaps where equipment had once been stored. "Whatever was here, we're too late. Just."

"How do you know?"

"Because these footprints are still fresh. And you can see that all this dust has only just been disturbed," Alex said.

They looked around. Gunfire continued, closer now.

Alex checked the schematics. "There's an air vent."

"Where?"

"Around here," he said, leading through a door to internal offices until—the wall ahead was rubble, some of it still hot from explosives.

"It's completely blocked," Phoebe said. "We can't get out this way."

"I can hear Rick's guys. They're still holding them back!" Alex called, running ahead of his mother. "We have to try another way."

A massive blast rang out and Alex was sent flying backward.

ALEX'S NIGHTMARE

In a world of black, a bright light appears and I move towards it, stumbling. It isn't until I start running that I know I am unconscious.

I'm in the dream world.

"It doesn't have to be like this," a metallic voice says.

I spin around but I can't see anyone. The voice is inside my head.

"You can be the one, Alex."

"Who are you?" I call out, but my voice just echoes and no answer comes back. I keep going towards a door, running flat out, but as fast as I run, the distance between me and the light behind the door remains the same.

I stop, waiting for the voice to go on.

"You can be the one—at the end. It's up to you. You will have the choice, and you should take it."

ALEX

Alex blinked his eyes. Phoebe was next to him, wrapping his right arm in a bandage.

"What? Where—?" he asked, sitting up, groggy.

"Slowly, slowly," Phoebe said. "We're in one of the medical labs. I don't know what happened on the other side of that door, but whoever it was decided to cut their losses and leave."

"Probably Stella, but it could even have been Solaris," Rick added, leaning over Alex and smiling. "I think we just had a narrow escape, in any case."

"What happened to my arm?" Alex said. "I just remember the blast and then . . ."

"You got knocked out, but you'll be OK," Phoebe said. "The good news is that a bit of metal tore into your arm—"

"That's *good* news?" Alex interrupted.

"It is, because it helped us find this," Phoebe said,

showing him a tiny piece of plastic and metal the size of a vitamin pill. A little red light sat at one end.

"It had been implanted in your arm," she said.

"You *what?*"

"My best guess would be that Stella put it there at some point when she was bringing you to the Enterprise," Phoebe said angrily. "While you were out, I removed it."

Alex thought back to when he'd first met Stella—at the hospital in New York.

She knocked me out when I tried to escape. Must have done it then.

"Do you think she did that just to me? Could she or any of the others have bugged anyone else?"

"We'll have to get everyone checked out," Phoebe said, sending messages through to the Academy and the Enterprise.

"Oh man, do you think that's how they always seem to know where Sam is?"

"Could be," Rick grimaced.

"We have to warn them," Alex said.

SAM

Sam woke up with a start. The storm was still lashing the island and the roof above them was leaking badly but managing to hold. Chris and Maria were somehow sound asleep. Sam rolled over and realized that the rock he thought he was sleeping on was in fact the dart gun.

Well, shooting myself in the foot would have helped me to get some sleep, I guess.

Sam smiled in his semiconscious delirium and put the dart gun to one side. He stretched out and changed his Stealth Suit to a padded, waterproof outfit similar to the snow suit he'd worn at the Academy's Swiss campus. In moments, he was back asleep.

SAM'S NIGHTMARE

It's hot and bright. Through narrowed eyes I look around and see sand dunes stretching out in every direction. I am marooned in a desert. There's nothing in sight—no buildings or vehicles or even a tree.

"Great," I say to myself, taking off my shirt and tying it around my head to block out some of the sun's blinding rays. "Middle of nowhere."

I trudge on, down dunes, up dunes, eyes fixed on a high ridge that I head towards.

At the bottom of a ravine is a dark patch of ground that I dig at and it soon pools with a tiny puddle of water. I crouch down on my hands and knees and sip it.

No.

Salty.

I sit back, resting for a moment.

"Sam! Sam!"

Someone is calling me.

The voice comes down from above somewhere, the sound echoing around me in this gully.

I get to my feet and climb as fast as I can. I stand at the top of the dune and listen . . .

"Sam?"

I know the voice—it's my father. I turn around and see my mom and dad on the dune behind me, like they've been following my fading footprints in the sand.

"Sam!" my mom says, waving.

I run towards them, my exhaustion forgotten. As I reach the top of the dune, my smile and enthusiasm wane and are replaced with panic.

My parents aren't there anymore.

I look all around—they are nowhere to be seen. I call for

them, but no reply comes. I look at the sand at my feet and see only my own footprints.

A mirage?

"Sam!"

I turn. There, a few dunes over in the direction of the ridge, my parents wave me over.

I run again.

Down, up, down, up, until I crest the dune where my parents are, and double over to catch my breath.

"Sam!"

I look ahead–they are still six or seven dunes away, towards the ridge. I look back the way I've come. My footprints are everywhere, like I've been wandering around this one dune for hours. I look up at my parents–

Gone.

"Sam?"

They are back the other way. A *long* way away.

"OK . . ." I say. "I know what this is. Let's change it up."

There is a crackle in the sky, lightning and then–

I am standing at the ridge and next to me are my parents.

"Hey," my father says. "That was neat."

"Yeah," I say, dusting the sand off myself.

"Getting good at this dreaming thing," my mom says.

"At last," I admit. "Where are we?"

"It's *your* dream," my father replies.

I look around. The sand dunes are gone and from the ridge I can see a canyon. "We've been here before," I say.

We are at a lookout I'd been to with my parents when I was ten.

"The Grand Canyon," my mother says. "Remember our trip here?"

I nod, then turn to them.

"Where are you guys?" I say. "Right now, I mean."

"We're here," they reply.

"In the Grand Canyon?" I say.

"Yep."

"Why?"

"It's where she took us," my mom says slowly.

"Who?" My heart starts to thump in my chest.

Neither answers. Then I see her.

Stella.

She stands by a car, holding a gun.

"Why are we here?" I ask.

My parents still don't answer.

"Why didn't you tell me you worked for the Enterprise?" I say.

Again they are silent. I turn to face them and they are gone once more.

I wait, expecting them to reappear somewhere near, on another ridge or maybe the dunes will return, but I am alone under Stella's glare, alone at the lookout, left with nothing but memories of my parents.

Stella too disappears into the heat haze of the desert landscape.

Now I am completely alone.

"Why?" I shout at the sky. "Why didn't you ever tell me?"

The ground underfoot shakes and the sky changes. It starts to rain but then I realize that it is me, crying, and I wake up.

SAM

Sam was warm. He stretched out and woke, his body slowly coming online. He looked around and saw—*sand?*

I'm on the island . . . it was just a dream about my parents. No, not parents, Enterprise Agents.

He shook off the thoughts and sat up.

Then he saw feet. In boots.

Sam reached out for his dart gun. In one swift move he snapped up and aimed straight for—

"Sam, no!"

"*Tobias?*"

Sam sat up further and looked around. The shelter was gone. Behind Tobias stood a contingent of Guardians.

"Maria?" he said to Tobias. "Where are Maria and her father?"

"They're at their camp, along with Rapha and Xavier."

"Huh?"

Then Sam realized. He was still on the same island, just no longer at the shelter with Maria and Chris.

"Did I . . . did I sleepwalk here?"

"Looks that way," Tobias said then laughed. "There's another talent we can add to your expanding skill set."

Sam realized he was on the sandbar, and Maria's boat, the *Scaramanga*, was tied up just in front of him.

"How did you guys all get here? What happened to the coast guards?"

"Thanks to the Guardian's call to the Academy, the Professor had some friends from the Dreamer Council put pressure on the Cuban government."

"So then?"

"They sent out the police to arrest those taking bribes from Hans. They missed out on apprehending Hans himself, unfortunately," Tobias said, then he pointed offshore. "But, as long as we're in Cuban waters, we've got a Cuban navy escort."

A gunboat was moored just off the island, flying the Cuban flag.

"How'd you do with those cannons?"

Tobias laughed. "You know, it was pretty impressive. Might have been a pirate in a past life."

"Sam!" Maria ran towards him, with the others close behind, and she hugged him. "We thought you'd been taken in the night."

"Apparently I sleepwalk now," Sam said.

Rapha and Xavier crowded around and Maria showed them the Gear that she'd found on the hidden galleon.

"Excellent," Tobias said. "OK, let's pack up and head to the boat."

"Where are we headed, back to London?" Sam said.

"The Florida Keys, actually, where we'll connect to a flight to Canada."

"Canada?" Sam said, as the group walked across the beach towards the *Scaramanga*. "What's in Canada?"

"Canadians," Xavier replied.

Sam smiled.

"We've got a team in Vancouver now," Tobias said. "And they're moving in on Lora and Eva's position."

"You've found them?"

"We've had confirmation that they're fine. Mac has them in a compound there."

"And how do we bust them out?" Sam asked.

Tobias turned to the huge captain of the Guardians next to him, who smiled and said in a broad Australian accent, "With brute force, mate. With brute force . . ."

Key West was an explosion of sound and vivid Technicolor to Sam, who'd grown used to the calm of the ocean and the constant low thrumming of the boat's engine on the way there. It was busy with cars and people and tourists—business as usual.

Little do they know the race going on to save them all . . .

Sam watched the world flash by as they hurried from the marina in a four-vehicle convoy: he, Maria, Xavier, Rapha, Tobias and Chris in a van with a couple of Guardians, the rest of the Guardians loaded into sedans surrounding them as they drove through the streets.

"Why are we driving?" Sam asked.

"Flight leaves from another island," Tobias replied, watching out his window. "Maybe we'll even drive across to the mainland."

"Why?" Sam asked. "Aren't we safer in the air?"

"We're safest when we change up our plans at the last minute," Tobias replied, "when we're unpredictable. Then those against us don't have time to plan their attack."

"Makes sense . . ." Sam said. He'd lost count of the times

that their enemies seemed to be too close for comfort—
or worse, there a step ahead of them. Sam knew that
somehow they had advance knowledge of the movements
of Dreamers and Academy personnel. "Maybe next time
we shouldn't have any plans at all."

"We've got safe houses set up all over," Tobias said. "If
we're lost or separated at all, the Guardians will take you
to the nearest one."

Sam glanced out to see the neighborhood streets had
ended and they were headed over a bridge, long and
smooth, stretching out far over the water. He marveled
at this feat of engineering, of man over nature, before
focusing back on the conversations around him.

". . . rescue Lora and Eva," Tobias continued.

"Where?" Xavier said.

"Vancouver. And we've seen that Alex is there too."

"So we're all going?" Sam said, pointing to Xavier,
Rapha, Maria and Chris.

Tobias looked at them. "No," he said. "Another new plan.
We'll form three separate teams, each with Guardians for
protection, and split up."

"Split up?" Xavier said.

"Drive, fly, you name it. Spread the chase, see if we can
distract our pursuers, at least for a while. Buy you and me
a little time to do what we need to, off the grid."

Sam nodded. "So we drive across the US?" he asked.

"For now," Tobias replied.

"I like road trips," Sam said as they drove down the road.

"Good—we've got a long one ahead of us," Tobias replied.

"What makes you so sure that there are enemies close by?" Maria asked.

"Because they will know that we've been in the field," Tobias said. "They will know that we'll likely head to the US. And we just can't take any chances—they're always just a step or two behind us."

"And they'll know," Sam said, "that we've found the next Gear. Right?" He instinctively looked to Maria.

Sam looked out the window and for a moment the image of his parents at the Grand Canyon from his dream flashed into his mind. He blinked it away.

Outside, the car behind, a white SUV with blacked-out windows, pulled alongside to pass but slowed a little, keeping pace with their vehicle. The back window rolled down.

"Brake!" Sam yelled, and without hesitation their driver hit the brakes hard as he could.

From the SUV's open window a machine gun's muzzle thrust out, the bullets tearing up the road right where their front wheel would have been.

Sam could see the Guardians' cars in front had slowed and were now locked in a gun battle of their own with two more vehicles approaching from the other end of the bridge.